John B. Pratt

The Life and Death of Jamie Fleeman

Anatiposi

John B. Pratt

The Life and Death of Jamie Fleeman

Reprint of the original, first published in 1859.

1st Edition 2023 | ISBN: 978-3-38231-208-4

Anatiposi Verlag is an imprint of Outlook Verlagsgesellschaft mbH.

Verlag (Publisher): Outlook Verlag GmbH, Zeilweg 44, 60439 Frankfurt, Deutschland
Vertretungsberechtigt (Authorized to represent): E. Roepke, Zeilweg 44, 60439 Frankfurt, Deutschland
Druck (Print): Books on Demand GmbH, In de Tarpen 42, 22848 Norderstedt, Deutschland

THE

LIFE AND DEATH

OF

JAMIE FLEEMAN

THE LAIRD OF UDNY'S FOOL

TWENTY-SIXTH THOUSAND

REVISED

ABERDEEN

LEWIS AND JAMES SMITH

—

MDCCCLIX

JAMIE FLEEMAN.

LIFE AND DEATH

OF

JAMIE FLEEMAN.

INTRODUCTION.

THERE are more fools in the world than those publicly accounted such, and in the number many who would be highly offended were the least hint thrown out that their names stood on the list. Idiots or common fools, whose minds are so framed that it is difficult to determine whether the weak parts or the strong be the more conspicuous, generally view things through a medium peculiar to themselves, and think, speak, and act in a way distinct from the great mass of mankind. While other men allow the world to become acquainted with only the more rational part of their views, the fool reveals all that comes into his thoughts. Both rational men and idiots build castles in the air. The former are accounted wise because they conceal the airy fabrics ; the latter are esteemed fools, not because they allow their thoughts to run riot, but because they cannot conceal their vagaries from the public. The one may embark in the wildest

A

schemes, and pursue the most headlong course, and still be reckoned no fool; while the other may say many witty things, and do many rational deeds, and still the world will not account him wise, but will laugh at both his sayings and his doings, because he does not follow exactly the same track nor view circumstances in the same light as the multitude. But if the world laugh at the eccentricities of the fool, the fool, in revenge, seems to hold the notions of the world in derision: for while the more rational part of the community are carefully keeping in one common and beaten track, and, individually, would be quite unhappy were they to be singular in their manners and habits, the fool fearlessly bounds into a path of his own formation, and pursues his way through a kind of fictitious region, wherein he seems to find enjoyments of no ordinary nature, and beyond the ken of all ordinary men.

A century or two ago, a *professed* fool was considered a necessary appendage to every family of distinction. The primitive elements of his character were the knave—the idiot—the crazed madman. Wit combined with apparent stupidity, unbending fidelity mingled with reckless audacity, and a discriminating judgment concealed by a well-dissembled indifference, were indispensable ingredients in his composition. When the demand for family fools was great, the supply appears to have been most abundant. A curious Act of Parliament shows us that at one time it was necessary to confine the assumption of this character by legislative enactment. It was "ordainit that shireffs, baylyies, and officiars inquer at ilk court, *gif thair be ony that maks them fulis that are nocht;* and gif ony sic be fundyn, that thai be put in the king's warde, or in his yrnis, for thair trespas, als lang as thai haf ony gudes of their awin to leve upon; and fra thai haf nocht to leve upon, that thair eris be nalyt to the trone, or to ane uther tre, and cuttit of, and bannysit the cuntre ; and gif thairaftir thai be fundyn again, that thai be hangyt."* This laconic piece of legislation shows that the emoluments of a fool must have been considerable, since the number of persons feigning to be fools was such as to call forth so severe an enactment. This is farther evident from a passage in Dunbar's poem, entitled " Kennedy's Testament : "—

> " To Jock the fule, my follie free,
> Lego post corpus sepultum.
> In faith I am mair fule than he,
> Licet ostendi bonum multum.
> Of corn and cattle, gold and fee,
> Ipse habet valde multum ;
> And yet he bleirs my Lordis ee,
> Fingendi eum fore stultum."

Thus it would appear that of their foolishness part was real and part was feigned. They were, generally, at least as much knaves as fools, concealing their knavery under that best of all cloaks—simplicity. Their dry sarcastic humour and rude ready wit received much freshness and zest from their wild craziness. They were a link between the quiet helpless idiot and the boisterous madman. They shared of the eccentricity of the latter and of the stupidity of the former, and added to these the sharp-wittedness of the knave. They are now almost, if not altogether, extinct. The fool's cap and bells have long hung untenanted on the walls, his seat by his lord on the *dais* has long since disappeared, and it is many a day since his sallies have been heard in the hall or at the festive board. The country clachan has still its innocent or idiot, and the crazed madman still wanders restlessly through his chosen dis-

* Act for the away-putting of Fenyet Fules, &c. 19th January 1449.—THOMSON's " Acts of Parliament of Scotland," vol. i.

trict; but it would seem as if these also were soon to disappear. Already they are much less frequently to be seen than formerly, being concealed from the public eye in the cells of charitable asylums. But till within these few years, we have seen several idiots led about the streets of Aberdeen, or wandering to and fro under their own guidance. We recollect one in particular—a most pitiful spectacle—who was led from door to door of the suburbs by a woman, we believe his mother. "Feel Peter," "Willie More," and many others, will be remembered by the youngest of our readers. In a country village it is no uncommon sight still to see, on a sunny day, the *innocent* seated bareheaded on the stone seat by the house door, or sitting for hours as motionless as a pillar, or wandering about, sometimes carrying on an unmeaning soliloquy, and sometimes running over the air of a favourite song. The race of madmen continued to appear on our streets to a later date. Indeed, we believe "Mourican-roum-roum-roum" has not discontinued his visits to the present hour. The backs of some of our juvenile readers, we doubt not, will be ready to attest how lately "Jean Carr" brandished her staff, and, single-handed, scoured the streets of a whole schoolful of her tormentors; while the bodies of some of them, perhaps, still ache at the memory of a direful conflict with that renowned amazon, "Lady Leddles."

It was in the fifteenth and sixteenth centuries that family fools were most in request. Before the eighteenth century, about the middle of which Jamie Fleeman flourished, matters wore a very different aspect. Jamie was perhaps the *ultimus Romanorum*, the last of the race of Scottish family fools—a class of beings which the author of *Waverley* has rendered so familiar to every one by his picture of "Daft Davie Gellatly." Jamie differed from his brethren and ancestors in this, that whereas the great majority of them were " fenyet fules," he was, in most respects, naturally what he appeared to be, and by chance fell into the very situation in which he was capable of acting a conspicuous part.

———

CHAPTER II.

PARENTAGE AND BOYHOOD.

THE author of the Biographical Sketch of Fleeman which appeared in the number of the *Aberdeen Magazine* for March 1832, candidly admits that his account of the fool was very imperfect, and in some respects not very correct. This was owing not to any design or inability on the part of the author, but to the scantiness of his materials and the channels of his information. With regard to Jamie's birth, his words are—" Mr James Fleming was born, as far as can now be ascertained, early in the last century. The place of this great man's birth is so uncertain, that the eighty-and-one parishes of Aberdeenshire may, if they please, contend for that high honour, in like manner as the seven cities of Greece contended for the glory of having been the birthplace of Homer." There is, however, no such uncertainty in the case. Jamie Fleeman first saw the light in the parish of Longside and braeside of Ludquharn. There are many still alive who can point out the spot where his parents lived, and still more who can tell how his mother was drowned, near the bridge of Ludquharn, in a deep pool, which at this very day is known by the name of " Fleeman's Pot." He had a brother who was killed on board one of his Majesty's ships, we believe the *Serapis;* and it was not till the beginning of the present century that his sister, Martha,* died at Nether Kinmundy, in the parish where she was born.

An association of ideas depends, in many instances, on the most trifling circumstances; and to imagine that the same effect will be produced, or the same interest excited, by any other means, is a mistaken notion. We are of opinion that Jamie's biographer has erred, in these respects, with regard to his hero's surname. There is not one who remembers Jamie that would recognise his old friend by the appellation of "Mr Fleming," or even "James Fleming." He was universally known, and is still mentioned, by the name of "Jamie Fleeman," a name possessing a charm sufficient, even at the present day, to arrest the attention of every child in the district of the country which Jamie frequented.

From the way in which the biographer has introduced his narrative, one would be led to suppose that Jamie was more "knave than fool," or, in other words, that he was a

---

* Having mentioned Martha, and it being improbable that any one now alive can be narrowly concerned in the matter, it may not be out of place to relate that she too had a kind of craze as well as her brother, but of a different kind. Martha's was of a religious turn. She was a Presbyterian of the old stamp ; and believing that quotations from Scripture were the best seasonings of common conversation, and the strongest proof of being a chosen vessel, the good woman had a text ready for every occasion. Once on a time her daughter (and be it known that Martha Fleeman was a woman of irreproachable character, and twice regularly married) having fallen among rather low company, on the evening of a market at Longside, the ill-natured women of the neighbourhood alleged that the maiden's fair fame was somewhat darkened. Soon after they were surprised by Martha running from house to house, and saluting each goodwife in the words of the prophet —"Rejoice not against me, O mine enemy ; when I fall I shall arise ; when I sit in darkness, the Lord shall be a light unto me."

fool by profession more than by nature. From the ample information which we have derived from those who were personally acquainted with Jamie, we can scarcely allow that this was really the case. Although he possessed wit keen as a razor, and sufficient understanding to take care of himself, yet he certainly had many of the properties peculiar to an idiot. His countenance, indescribably or even painfully striking, wore that expression which at once betrays the absence of sound judgment. His head large and round—his hair, perhaps naturally brown, but rendered, by constant exposure to the weather, of a dingy foxcolour, and not sleek, but standing on end, as if poor Jamie had been frightened out of his wits—indicated that his foolishness was not assumed but real. In a word, his general appearance, his manner and habits, combined to excite the suspicion that, although the lamp of reason was ever and anon bursting forth in brilliant flashes of wit, yet its light was flickering and unsteady. The lurid gloom which generally prevailed tended to render those bright gleams more attractive than they otherwise might have been, and invested them with an unnatural sort of character, which riveted attention, and at the same time amused and amazed the beholder.

The author of the Biographical Sketch has stated that, "either from necessity, or from that love of animals so common to persons of weak intellect, Jamie's bed was in the dog-kennel among the hounds." We have inquired into the correctness of this statement, and have found that although Fleeman generally invited the dog to share his bed, there is yet no reason to conclude that he ever passed a single night in a dog-kennel. There are many who allow dogs to sleep in their bedrooms, perhaps in their beds, who would be very unwilling to admit that they were in the habit of sleeping in a dog-kennel. The place where a dog sleeps may perhaps be termed a kennel; but still, when we speak of a dog-kennel, our meaning is commonly confined to a place set apart for the habitation of dogs; and therefore an erroneous opinion is apt to be conveyed, when it is said of Fleeman that "his bed was in the dog-kennel among the hounds."

Jamie spent the days of his boyhood about the house of Sir Alexander Guthrie, commonly known in the country by the appellation of "the Knight of Ludquharn," and, at a very early period of life, began, by bluntness of manner and shrewdness of remark, to attract the notice of his betters. On account of these peculiarities, young Fleeman was permitted to take liberties which, in other boys, would have been rigorously repressed; and being introduced to the company which commonly visited at Ludquharn, he never failed to contribute to their amusement, and to ingratiate himself into their favour. Hence the reason that, when Ludquharn no longer afforded him a home, he found an open door, and, it may be said, a ready welcome, at every gentleman's mansion which he chose to visit in the neighbourhood.

CHAPTER III.

ATTACHMENTS AND PREJUDICES.

RARELY is a fool pleased with a common dress, and the dress which Jamie Fleeman chose to wear was not of usual pattern. With regard to inexpressibles, accounts do not well agree, some admitting that he patronised the modern form of garment, but most declaring that he was partial to the more ancient and upland fashion, and decked himself out in a blue-baize petticoat.   Be this as it may, it is certain that a kind of sackcloth doublet, in place of a coat and vest, served to protect his upper man from the weather.   As to his head, it had no acquaintance with hat, cap, or bonnet ; and his feet were in much the same state of slender intimacy with shoes.   If his appearance was calculated to attract notice, his tone of voice was not less so.   It was peculiar to himself—hollow, loud, nasal; so that, while his words dropped slowly from his lips, or rather were trumpeted through his nose, and at the same time were accompanied by an air of Scottish simplicity or cunning waggery (no one could well have said which), it was next to impossible to be inattentive to his singular remarks and sarcastic witticisms.

Fools are rarely without feelings both of affection and of hatred, and in general these are of a very marked description.   It may be supposed that Jamie's attachments, when once fixed, were strong and unwavering ; and an instance corroborative of this is recorded.   When Sir Alexander's family was about to leave the old mansion at Ludquharn, one of the ladies broadly hinted to Fleeman that they would be under the necessity of dispensing with his services, alleging as their reason that they were henceforth to occupy a smaller house, and were compelled by various circumstances to part with every servant whose labour was not absolutely necessary.   Jamie listened with downcast look and heavy heart ; and having some indistinct notion that the worthy ladies were under the necessity of curtailing their comforts on account of limited means of subsistence, and believing that his services might be of some use to them in their humbler station, he generously resolved to

convince them that, to him, worldly considerations were of
no value in comparison to the regard which he had for his
friends.   In a faltering tone, which showed that the poor
creature was really affected, he stammered out,—" Ye hae
been kind, kind to me, an' I canna leave you in your strait.
I'm gain' wi' you, should ye gang to *the ill pairt*." *   The
effect of this speech may be gathered from the following
kind reply :—" Well, I believe, Jamie, we have few friends
who would venture so far with us, so we must do something for you."   Even fools may in some things set an example to wiser men ; and we have here, in a poor simple-
ton, an instance of sincere gratitude and noble disinter-
estedness which would embellish any character, and which
many might be proud to reckon in the list of their virtues.
There are numbers who may perhaps laugh at the singular argument which Fleeman used to prove the regard he
felt for the family of Ludquharn ; but while they ridicule
the odd language of the fool, let them consider his conduct on the occasion, and haply they may find in it something which commands their respect and deserves their imi-
tation.

Jamie was recommended to the Laird of Udny, about
whose hand he spent many a day ; but as far as we can
learn, he was at full liberty to go and come, just as he liked
and when he thought proper—a liberty of which he not
unfrequently availed himself.   After saving the charter-
chest at Knockhall, Udny allowed him a peck of meal and
sixpence a-week during his life.   There was likewise some
mention made of a pair of shoes once a-year, but on this part
of his reward he did not very scrupulously insist.   Most
people discover a pretty strong memory in cases where a
promise advantageous to themselves has been made ; and

* The infernal regions.

in this respect, at least, Fleeman was like other men. That he did not wholly forget the shoes which had been promised, we gather from the following anecdote :— Having some wish to get a new doublet, he seated himself on the opposite side of a dyke from that along which he saw Udny approaching, and, as if unconscious of the Laird being near, he began to sing with all his might,—" I'm to get a new coat frae bonny Udny ; I'm to get a new coat frae bonny Udny." The Laird listened for some time to this simple and rather unique ditty, when, looking over the dyke, he said,—" Well, Fleeman, ye shall have a new coat." " What ! and sheen tee ?" inquired Jamie. The laird smiled and assented.

Fidelity towards those whom they esteem is a trait generally found in the character of fools. They cannot bear to hear anything to the reproach of their favourites ; and when intrusted by them with any charge, they seem to have a pride in executing it with fidelity and precision. Such was the confidence placed in Fleeman by Lady Mary Hay of Erroll,* that, when he was at the castle, she rarely took any other servant with her when she rode from home. Jamie was extremely proud of such distinguished honour, and her ladyship ran no risk of annoyance from any one while he was her attendant. Fourscore years ago, it was not as it is at the present day with regard to travelling. No turnpike roads then intersected the country, and it was only on extraordinary occasions that any one thought of travelling in a carriage. When Lady Mary had occasion to go to Aberdeen, she mounted her steed, while Jamie, astride on a stick, ran on before. When they reached Waterside he usually kept his face towards his mistress, and, wading the Ythan back foremost, every now and

* Not the Countess, as mentioned in the first edition.

then called out, " Your ladyship has nae got afore me yet, I think." He would then laugh most heartily, as if he had done or said something very wonderful.

From the indulgence he met with, and the privilege usually granted to fools, he sometimes took the liberty, as we have already mentioned, of doing and saying things to those with whom he resided which no other person durst have taken. James, Earl of Erroll, had procured a superior breed of cows. His lordship praised them so highly, that his brother, the Hon. Charles Boyd, then residing at Ludquharn, became particularly anxious to have some of the breed. The Earl would not part with the cows, even to his brother, but at an exorbitant price; but this being at last agreed to, four of the number were transferred from Slains Castle to Ludquharn. Whether the change of pasture had had any bad effect on the cows, or whether they had been more famous for stock than for milk, or whether any other cause might have been assigned, is a matter which cannot now be explained ; but so it was, that they had not been many weeks at Ludquharn when complaints began to be heard about the quantity of milk which they yielded, and surmises were quietly hazarded that the Earl had cheated his brother. Fleeman was at the time paying a visit to his old quarters, and very soon understood that the cows were not only not answering the high expectations which had been formed concerning them, but that they did not yield a quantity of milk sufficient to supply the family, and therefore could not be kept much longer about the place. Whether or not any hints more direct were given to Fleeman is unknown ; but one fine night in the beginning of harvest, Jamie, after all the people about Ludquharn had retired to rest, stole quietly to the byre, and, having unloosed the cows, was soon past Cairn Cattach,

with them before him. Arriving at Slains Castle long
before daybreak, he got the cows under Lord Erroll's bedroom window, when he began to yell and swear among
them as if he had been in a violent passion. His lordship,
aroused from his slumbers, was much amazed at the unaccountable noise; but having got up and opened the
window, he discovered Fleeman. Still his surprise was by
no means removed, when by means of the dim moonlight
he saw several cows crowded under the window, and Jamie
keeping them there with much noise and trouble. "What
do you want, Fleeman? What is the meaning of this?"
demanded his lordship. "Ye canna thrive, my lord," answered Jamie — "ye canna thrive, my lord. Ye hae
cheated your brother Charlie. Ye hae gi'en him kye as
dry as the bull, an' I hae brought them to get the milk
from your lordship that ye said they had when in your
aught. Ye hae kept the milk to yoursel', my lord. Ye
canna thrive. Ye hae cheated your brother Charlie." And
then, suddenly breaking off the conversation, he muttered
in a low tone of voice, "D——d yule rumps." His lordship
ordered him to put the cows into the byre until morning,
when he would settle the matter. Jamie did so, but
stayed not to hear his lordship's decision. He was at Ludquharn by the time the domestics got up, when, as may be
supposed, there was no small stir about the cows. They
were everywhere sought, but could nowhere be found. No
one could tell or even conjecture what had become of
them. Fleeman was profoundly silent on the subject till
Mr Boyd was informed of the inexplicable circumstance,
when, in a peculiarly grave and ludicrous tone, he said,
"Faith, the kye are maybe awa for their milk that they
left at the castle." Being farther interrogated, he merely
replied, "I'll wager an ounce o' tobacco, Erroll has ta'en

back his yule kye, an' ordered them into his byre. Keep
ye the price, if ye're a wise man."

Fleeman was a man of strong prejudices. These had
respect to places, persons, and animals, and were often
taken up, one could scarcely have said how, but always
maintained with a degree of determination not a little uncommon. Sometimes his prejudices were in favour of the
object, and sometimes the reverse.

There are perhaps few things in the world about which
men are more capricious than about the beauties and properties of local situations. One generally discovers, in the
place where he has spent his early days, charms which any
other person would, in all probability, never find out ;
and instances may be found of men who are loud in praise
of situations which, to the cursory observer, are both bleak
and uninteresting. It is not to be supposed that we can
give any good reason for Fleeman's partiality to some
places in preference to others. We can merely state the
fact, that he showed such partiality. In his way to Slains
Castle, he very frequently called and staid a few days at
the Nethermill of Cruden, a place of whose beauties and
situation he had so high an opinion, that it was a common
saying of his, " Guid faith, the king must be a great fool,
or he would come and stay at the Nethermill."

With regard to persons, Jamie's prejudices were of a
very singular character. Prejudices have generally some
connection with the merits or demerits of the esteemed or
hated object. Fleeman's had none. Whole classes of the
community, and not individuals, were the objects of his ill-
will. Some trifling and accidental circumstance not unfrequently gave a bias to his opinion. If a woman had a
head adorned with the golden locks so much admired by
the ancients, no more was needed to reduce her very low

in Fleeman's estimation. "Where saw ye ever a lady wi' scarlet hair?" he would growl, and no other reason would he give for his ill-founded prejudice. The cause was probably connected with the following circumstance :—There was at Waterton a cook-maid whose locks were of the above-mentioned colour. This maiden had a temperament not of the mildest kind ; and when poor Fleeman had in any degree been negligent of his duty, she would have sworn in the most furious way, and wished him in a bad place. Jamie stood more in awe of the cook than he did of any other person about a gentleman's house. Although he often deeply grumbled, yet these indications of rebellion were generally displayed in an indirect way, and just as he was marching off to obey the order against which he was complaining. Thus his expressions of rebellion were always neutralised by his acts of obedience. It must be allowed, however, that Fleeman had no good-will towards the whole race of cook-maids. He respected their commands more from a dread of their resentment than from a wish to oblige them. Wherever he went, they insisted on having a right to his services, and would give him nothing to eat unless he kept plenty of peats and water about their hands. One day Jamie had allowed either the one or the other of these necessary articles to be wanting. Complaints concerning his negligence were louder than usual, and threats of no ordinary portent were uttered in his hearing. These were continued so long, that Fleeman's anger began to be a little excited, and, his patience being completely exhausted, he ventured to reply in a manner more direct than usual. This new species of offence greatly increased the rage of the maid, and she wished him in h—ll for his impudence, as she had formerly wished him with its monarch for his carelessness. "I see your drift, you jade,"

said Jamie. " You expect to be there yoursel', and to tor-
ment me wi' your eternal cry of ' Peats, peats, Fleeman ;'
and ' Water, water, Fleeman.' There is an old boy there
already that will hold peats eneuch about your hand. As
for water, ye may cry till your jaws split, but there will be
nane for your use." From that day forward the maidens
with golden locks were objects of his aversion. The anecdote is perhaps one of the least proper for public notoriety;
but as it brings into view a leading feature of Fleeman's
character, its impropriety is not so great as to demand its
suppression.

It was a trait in Fleeman's character, that he watched
every opportunity to annoy those whom he did not like,
and often adopted means for this purpose as singular as
they were sure. Factors were no favourites with Jamie.
In this case, too, the tide of his prejudice set strongly
against the whole race. One day a proprietor, at whose
house Jamie was staying, was walking out with his factor, and showing him a field of hill-land which he had
cultivated at considerable expense, but which had proved
very unproductive.—" I have," said the gentleman, " tried
many things in this field, but have succeeded in none,
and I know not what to put in it that would thrive. I
should be glad, Mr ——, to have your advice with regard
to the matter." As sometimes happens, the man of business was not very intelligent in anything with regard to
farming but the collection of the rents. Yet, unwilling to
be thought ignorant, he put on an air of great consequence,
and mused for a time, as if about to give a very sage and
useful advice. In the mean time, Jamie, who was near, was
overheard saying, " Od, I could tell you what would thrive
in't."—" Well, Fleeman," said the laird, " and what might
that be ?"—" Plant it wi' factors," said the fool; " they

thrive in every place ; but for all that," added he, " d—l curse the crop if it be very profitable." Both the laird and the factor were covered with confusion.

Among the crowd of mortals there are not a few whose minds are so framed that they appear to place all eminence in some trifling circumstance. Fleeman occasionally betrayed some symptoms of this singular disposition. For example, if he heard any one performing on the bagpipes, he almost invariably marched up to him, and bluntly asked, " Can ye play the Piper's Maggot ? " * If the musician replied that he could play the tune, Fleeman would immediately request him to do so, and then he would extol him as an excellent piper, although, perhaps, the most bungling performer imaginable ; while, on the other hand, whatever the musician's merits might have been, if he unfortunately could not play the favourite air, he was at once degraded in the fool's estimation, who would henceforth report him as one not worthy of the least share of public approbation. " He a piper !" Fleeman would say ; " he's a bummer ; he canna play the Piper's Maggot ! "

Jamie had a prejudice in favour of dogs and in hatred of cats, and this, he said, was " *gentlemanny.*" All the curs in the country knew him well, and were glad to see him. Wherever he stayed much, the dog was generally permitted to share his bed and board. At Waterton, it is said that he had taught a large house-dog to observe a line drawn across the pottage pot. On one side of the line, the pottage belonged to Jamie ; on the other the dog was permitted to feed. The cur knew, from experience, that Jamie's spoon made the boundary to be duly respected. As the story has it, the dog was from

* The name of an old Scotch air.

home one morning, when Jamie's acquaintance, the cook, insisted that the cat should be permitted to occupy his place. It was plainly revealed by Fleeman's side-long look and heavy brow that he did not much relish this new messmate. He did not, however, venture to remonstrate, and the maid placed her cat opposite to Jamie. Poor puss, ignorant of the laws observed in the domain of the pottage pot, speedily transgressed, by putting her nose across the marches. Jamie viewed her for a moment with an eye of sovereign contempt. He even suspended his own operations for a short space, that he might quietly observe an act of such daring aggression. Perceiving in the cat no signs of either fear or shame on account of the extraordinary encroachment, he deemed it a crime of too grave a nature to be punished in the usual way, by a slap on the aggressor's face with the back of his spoon ; so, quietly slipping his hand down on the enemy's head, he with a sudden jerk forced her nose as far as the ears among the scalding posset, gravely remarking, "Desperate diseases require desperate cures, ye d—d wretch." It was some time, and cost some pains, before the cook got her favourite cat well again ; but whether Curry* was at home or not, she never after proposed puss as a messmate to Fleeman.

There are in the world many who, from their endeavours to appear great, render themselves very ridiculous. The truly great and honourable keep from disgraceful and low actions, and are never afraid of their dignity from humble conduct and good-natured condescension ; while those who would be thought great, but whose claims to such distinction are founded on pride rather than merit, and on impudence rather than good sense,

* Courage, the dog's name.

are afraid of every action which would place them on an apparent level with humble though honest men, and would consider their dignity compromised and their honour at stake, were they to treat those who are poorer, or who have been less fortunate than themselves, with any degree of attention or common civility. We have rarely met with an instance where such silly pride met with a severer rebuff than it once received from Fleeman. Jamie being at a harvest-home, the farmer's daughter, a young maiden of lively disposition, and fond of a little innocent frolic, invited him to dance with her. Fleeman, proud of being so honoured, or rather, perhaps, anxious to show his respect for the young lady, who was a great favourite, immediately stood up, when her mother, thinking that the whole family would be disgraced by the maiden's frolic with Jamie, interfered and prohibited her from proceeding with the dance. While she was scolding her daughter for her imprudence and low behaviour, as she was pleased to term it, some of the party endeavoured to mitigate her rage, and to convince her that there would not have been much harm in it, even had her daughter danced a reel with Jamie. "Let the auld owman alone," said Jamie, with a most sarcastic air : "say nothing more about her ; she is God's handiwork." We have doubts whether the bitter sarcasm in this remark will be generally apprehended. To give some explanation of its meaning, it may be remarked that, when any person is naturally weak in mind or deformed in body, in speaking of such a one, the common people say, "He is God's handiwork ; " which means that there is some great blemish, and that it would be improper to say much about it, seeing it is the work of nature rather than the fault of the individual. Fleeman's remark indicated that the gudewife's pride betrayed such imbecility of mind that rational people ought not to say much of the matter.

The author of the Biographical Sketch in the *Aberdeen Magazine* gives the following anecdote :—" The laird of Waterton, it is told, was held by Mr Fleeming in especial aversion.　One day, when Mr Fleeming was lolling on a bank of the Ythan, basking himself in the sun, he was hailed from the other side of the water by the laird, who asked him where was the best ford.　The malicious knave directed the laird to the deepest pool in the river, and the laird, attempting to cross it, narrowly escaped drowning. When he arrived, sorely drenched, on the other side, he made up to Mr Fleeming, and, in a voice hoarse with passion and cold water, accused the poor fool of a design to drown him.　'Gosh behere, laird !' said Mr Fleeming, 'I've seen the geese and the dyeucks, hunners o' times crossin' there ; and I'm sure your horse has langer legs than the dyeucks or the geese either.'"

This is not the edition of the story which is commonly told.　We have frequently heard the anecdote, but never learned that he hated the laird, or that he was the person whom Fleeman misinformed.　To his benefactors he was always faithful, and it is improbable that the laird could have been ignorant of the state of the river close to his own house.　Common report mentions a stranger on a visit at Waterton as the luckless wight.　This gentleman had made some ill-natured remarks respecting Jamie.

Fleeman, when intrusted with any message or secret, was never known to betray the confidence reposed in him. Nothing annoyed him more than inquiries whither he was going, or what he was about ; and many a one, who wished curiously to pry into matters with which he had no concern, met with such rebukes from Fleeman as were calculated to teach him better manners, and remind him to busy himself about his own affairs. The Countess of Erroll was well aware of Fleeman's fidelity in this respect, and not unfrequently intrusted him with messages which few so fit would have been found to carry. After Culloden, many of the country gentlemen who had joined the Prince's standard were lying concealed in the neighbourhood of their former dwellings. As the Countess had taken a very active part in advising all the gentlemen in the north, with whom she had the least influence, to espouse the young Adventurer's cause, so after the defeat of their darling project she continued to keep up a correspondence with as many of them as possible. She consulted their safety by every means she could devise, and as far as was practicable, administered to their immediate wants, while they lurked in the most sequestered spots, and were in continual danger of falling into the hands of those who scoured the country in quest of them. Fleeman was much employed by the Countess about this time. He could traverse the country without exciting suspicion, and he was capable not only of keeping a secret, but of evading the most searching examination, if any should have taken it into their heads to question him. Lord Pitsligo was at that time lying in close concealment at the house of Auchiries, in the parish of Rathen. The Countess of Erroll was well aware of this, and, as often as prudence rendered it advisable, sent in the most private manner to ask for the welfare of old Mr Brown,* and perhaps to correspond with him concerning his safety, or to inform him concerning the fate of his companions in distress. In going from Slains Castle to Auchiries, Jamie had to pass the house of a proprietor who was a deter-

---

* John Brown, the name assumed by Lord Pitsligo.

mined enemy to the Prince and all who favoured him. Fleeman was well aware of this, and, as may be supposed, bore the laird no good will. One morning, as he was on his way to Auchiries, this gentleman met him and abruptly accosted him, for the purpose of getting either a little amusement or a little information. " Where are you going, Jamie ?" " I'm gaun to hell, sir !" said Fleeman, dryly. This did not encourage farther speech, and the parties went their ways. In the evening, as Fleeman was returning, they chanced again to meet, when the gentleman took up the theme so suddenly laid down in the morning. " What are they doing at hell, Jamie ?" " Just fat they're deein' here, sir," answered Fleeman; " lattin' in the rich folk, an' keepin' out the peer." " What said the devil to you, Jamie ?" " Ou, he said na muckle to *me*, sir ; but he was speerin' sair about *you*." *

He who needlessly and wantonly commits mischief will rarely escape the punishment which such conduct deserves. A travelling pedlar, nicknamed "Berries," ventured on one occasion to play off an ill-natured joke at Fleeman's expense. It was the winter season, and Berries had taken up his quarters for a few days at Mill of Leask, in the parish of Slains. This was a half-way house of Fleeman's when passing from Waterton to Slains Castle ; and, as Mr Sangster and his family were great favourites of his, he often prolonged his visits for several days. Arriving at the house when Berries was there, one of the maid-servants asked him if he was hungry. " Ay, an' thirsty tee," answered Fleeman. In a few minutes, Jamie was busily employed in refreshing himself with bannocks and pork,

* The particulars connected with this anecdote have been kindly furnished by a very old person, who had seen what was printed in the second edition.

while the servant girl, at the desire of her mistress, prepared a drink of warm ale for his comfort, as he had come
in shivering with cold, the weather being excessively
stormy. Berries, among other small articles, carried pepper
for sale. Addressing Fleeman, he said, "'Od, Jamie, I
think your drink would warm you more if it had a little
black spice in it." Jamie assented, when, instead of *black
spice,* the malicious knave put in a considerable quantity
of *black rappee.* As Jamie's taste does not appear to have
been very nice, he drank off the beverage without making
any further remark than that Berries' spice had "a cursed
ill *knegum.*" * Drawing near the fire to warm himself and
dry his clothes, he soon began to feel very uneasy. The
strong potation began to give unequivocal indications that
it would not endure close confinement, while Berries perceiving such evident signs of the success of his trick, could
not contain himself, but burst out into an immoderate fit
of laughter. Fleeman was not in a state to seek for revenge
at that particular time. He vomited so excessively, that
no small alarm as to the consequences was excited. His
bed was prepared, however, and a more wholesome beverage administered, and before morning Fleeman was himself
again. The pedlar, when he saw that his joke had become
more serious than he anticipated, took a sudden departure,
no doubt dreading Jamie's ire, and perhaps apprehending
the severe reproofs of Mr Sangster and his family. Summer
came, and with it Aiky Fair, in which Berries had a flash-
ing stall of little "nick-nacks." Jamie was never in his
lifetime absent from Aiky Fair. He soon espied his old
acquaintance the pedlar, and as soon set about repaying
him with interest for his present of the black spice. Off
he set to John Barnet's tent, where he knew the recruiting

* A disagreeable flavour.

party always went a-dramming, and proposed to the
sergeant to find him a good recruit, on condition that he
himself might be allowed to enlist him, and to march before the party in full uniform. No sooner said than done.
Jamie was fully equipped,* and furnished with a shilling.
Off he marched, sword in hand, directly to Berries' stall,
while the shouts of "attention !—right about face !—quick
march !" rent the air. "Roll went the drum, and the
fife played cheerily," when the party, followed by a rear-
guard as motley as ever attended " the knight of the woful
countenance," reached the pedlar's stall. Fleeman gave
the word "halt." "Ou, Jamie," said Berries, "are ye
turned sodger ?"—"Ou, ay," quoth Jamie, "will ye list ?"
—"'Od, I dinna care though I list wi' you, Jamie," said
the pedlar, never suspecting anything serious. "Here's a
shilling, then, in the king's name and authority." The
pedlar thoughtlessly took the shilling, when Fleeman,
wheeling about, marched his party back to the tent where
he had left the sergeant. "Well, Jamie," said the sergeant,
"have you enlisted your man ?" "Hout ay have I, sergeant, come an' look at him," said Fleeman, in the greatest
glee imaginable. On their arrival at the stall, Berries, who
knew too well the tricks by which men were *trepanned*,
perceived at once that he had allowed himself to be duped.
The sergeant told him to dispose of his "all," and prepare
to join the party. In vain did the pedlar protest that it
was "all for fun" that he had taken the shilling. The
sergeant seriously told him that, as he had received the
king's money, he was to all intents and purposes enlisted.

* This was no uncommon occurrence. Some old people yet recollect
having seen Fleeman parading the streets of Peterhead, dressed partly
as a soldier. The recruiting party indulged and encouraged him in this,
as by this means young fellows were attracted to them.

" Nae jeukin now, Berries," quoth Fleeman, " ye maun just gang or pay *the smart ;* ye made me pay the smart last winter wi' a suddenty, ye mind ! " In short, the pedlar had to pay the money, which he did, with many an imprecation upon Fleeman, who gave such vent to his joy when he saw him pay down his guinea, that an immense crowd was attracted to the spot, and joined loudly in the laugh against the poor pedlar. As a parting salute, Fleeman roared out, in his own deep nasal tone, " Deevil care, Berries, that's for garrin' me drink the tobacco bree." *

CHAPTER IV.

FEATS OF STRENGTH.

THAT Jamie was possessed of uncommon bodily strength is sufficiently authenticated. Nature seems to have given him in powers of body for what she denied him in strength of mind. If he was inferior to many in the latter, he was

* About the time when Fleeman lived, common swearing, or low expressions partaking of the nature of cursing, were rather fashionable among the higher ranks of society, and, as a matter of course, sedulously imitated by thousands of those who moved in a lower sphere. This in some measure accounts for the frequent allusion to the arch fiend which we meet with in Fleeman's sayings. We would, however, put the young readers of this history in mind of the fact, that the practice of interlarding common conversation with oaths has become quite unfashionable in good society. Without reference to the immorality of the practice, the manners of the age are sufficient to induce every one who has any regard for the good opinion of the world to abstain from all low expressions and gross allusions. The manners of the present day are much more refined than were those of the middle of last century. Expressions were then tolerated, the use of which would now be esteemed incontestable evidence of low breeding and a coarse mind ; and they are completely banished from the more refined circles of society, and held in detestation by every one who has the least claim to politeness.

superior to most in the former. His figure indicated extraordinary strength, which his habits may have helped to
confirm. He was rather above the middle size, and very
broad between the tips of the shoulders; but the most
striking peculiarity of his form was its roundness. His chest
was not flattened even in an ordinary degree, and yet it
would be incorrect to say that he was deformed ; while the
singularly-shaped sackcloth or serge garment that he wore
left his neck and part of his breast completely bare ; and, by
this constant exposure of his body to the weather, his constitution seemed to be hardened and his strength increased.

It is not easy to determine whether Fleeman's uncommon sagacity or extraordinary strength was the more surprising, or whether his dry humour yielded to his acute
wit. Upon one occasion he was sent with a letter to the
laird, resident at that time in Edinburgh. Jamie arrived
in Edinburgh safely, but he was quite ignorant of the
laird's address, and this he set himself to work to discover.
As he wandered through the streets, he narrowly inspected
every dog he met, and he was at last sufficiently lucky to
recognise one of his old bed-fellows. Seizing him in his
arms, he ran into a shop, and seeing a coil of ropes measured off five or six yards, and fastening this round the
dog's neck set him down, and giving him a few hearty
kicks—" Hame wi' you, ye scunging tyke, hame !"—and
thus he discovered the laird's dwelling-place. As a proof
of his extraordinary strength, it is added that, though the
rope was what is called " plough-line," which, it seems, is
a very strong sort of rope, he instantly snapped it in two
with his hands—an exhibition of strength which so terri-
fied the shopkeeper that he allowed Jamie to take himself
off without asking for payment, or making any demur to
this felonious abduction of his wares.

Fleeman's affection for dogs was, in some measure, the means of saving the Laird of Udny's charter-chest, when the house of Knockhall was burned. On the night in question, Jamie had sat down on his bed, and was labouring in one department of his vocation, namely, boring and tuning a chanter or Scotch whistle, an instrument on which he could play a little, and with which he often amused himself. While thus employed, his friend the dog came and pulled at part of his dress. "Haud out by— swithe !" said Jamie, and drove him away. Fleeman now betook himself to sleep, but again the dog came, and would not allow him to rest. Jamie, at last, assuming a milder tone, said, " *Tyangie*, fat ails ye ? Ye're wantin' out, are ye ? Weel, weel, I'se eemer (I shall humour) you for ance." He opened the door, and discovered that the house was on fire. Immediately he ran and awoke the gardener, who was a very great favourite of his; then, rushing to the charter-room, the door of which the flames had already reached, he broke in, and taking the iron chest in his arms, dashed it through a window, whose framework was composed of oak. It is true what the author has said, that it required three ordinary men to lift the chest. During this time the gardener had given the alarm to the inmates of the house. By-and-by Jamie was observed gamboling and frisking about on the green, and apparently in great ecstasy of joy. This very much surprised the gardener and others who were present. At length Jamie's conduct attracted their attention in a particular manner ; for, as the raging element acquired strength, Jamie's expressions of delight became more lively. Those who were attracted by his oddities observed that he kept muttering something to himself, and they became anxious to learn what it was that gave him such delight. The gardener stole behind him, and heard the following sentence :—" She aye liket to be speaking o' hell, but faith she'll get hell at hame the night, and d—l care." It flashed like lightning upon the gardener's recollection, that he had forgot to awaken the housekeeper, and he knew that Fleeman's portentous words referred to the poor creature. This domestic was very much disliked by Jamie. Among other reasons of his hatred, one was, as he himself expressed it, " She gies me naething but doups o' candles to kitchen my meat." She was likewise somewhat ill-tempered, and often wished Jamie in warm quarters when he offered to complain of her parsimonious habits, or to resent her unkind treatment. The gardener was in the utmost distress about the object of Fleeman's abhorrence ; and Jamie's affection for the former overcame his hatred for the latter. When he saw his friend in trouble, and understood the cause, he merely remarked, " He disna ken the nature of the jade sae weel's I dee ;" and immediately he darted through the flames, already roaring at her bedroom door, and gave her the alarm—" Lucky ! Lucky ! ye auld —— ; rise, ye rotten rudas ! or ye'll get a pair o' het hurdies ere lang !"

There was in Aberdeen an English regiment, whose commanding officer was a gasconading fellow, and constantly bragging of the extraordinary strength of his men. One day the Laird of Udny and this officer were of the same party at dinner. When the glass began to circulate the officer began to boast, and, as usual, got louder and louder in praise of his men, as he became more and more heated with wine. At length Udny, believing that an insult was intended to his countrymen, said, rather smartly, " From all accounts, these famous grenadiers of yours are the best wrestlers that England can produce. I'll take you a wager of twenty guineas, that the lad who herds my cows, and carries peats and water to the kitchen, will throw the best man in your regiment." The officer was in a paroxysm of rage, but, confident that his men were as good as he had represented them to be, he readily took the bet, while he muttered an oath, that "the d—d pride of the Scotch would soon be laid as low as it was on Drummossie Muir. Impudence, forsooth! Compare a blackguard Scotch servant to the finest fellows that ever crossed the English border!" Time and place being appointed for the trial, Udny, after ordering his servant to buy half a pound of fine twist tobacco, set off for his residence. Fearing that Jamie might not relish the job, Udny thought it necessary to coax him a little ; and, knowing that he was passionately fond of tobacco, he presented the half pound, at the same time saying, "Fleeman, I have got myself into a scrape, and no man but you can take me out of it." Jamie, eyeing the tobacco with a look of great satisfaction, his lip curling into a kind of smile at seeing himself in possession of such a treasure, twisted off a couple of inches from the end of it, clapped it into his cheek, and looking Udny in the face, said, with an air of great seriousness, "Fat is't, sir?" "You must *shake a fa'* for me, Fleeman," replied Udny. "And is that a'?" said Jamie. "But it is with soldiers, Jamie ; and if ye throw them, ye shall get another half pound of tobacco," was Udny's reply. Jamie began to gambol and cut capers, as was his custom when in good humour. Udny had gained his point, as far as Jamie's consent and assistance were concerned. On the day appointed, Jamie was seen standing near the Cross, on the plainstones, dressed in the sackcloth coat which he usually wore. His head was bare, and his hair standing on end, as on ordinary occasions. The soldiers, not dreaming

that they jested with their antagonist, were playing him
all sorts of tricks, while Jamie sullenly kept his place, and
seemed to heed them not. When the hour approached,
the colonel appeared, and had his men drawn up in order.
Seeing no person with Udny, he asked, with an air of tri-
umph, whether he had forgot that he had promised to produce a cowherd who was to throw the best man that England could produce ? Udny beckoned to Jamie, who came
capering forward. The officer looked with an air of utter
contempt on Udny and his cowboy, while a broad laugh
burst from every soldier in the ranks, when he saw the
poor idiot, whom he had lately been jeering, brought
forward as a match for any man in the company. As the
soldiers were really fine men and expert wrestlers, their
commander, instead of selecting the strongest of his party,
ordered out one of the weakest, determined, as he thought,
to turn the laugh, as well as the bet, against Udny. But
it is sometimes easier to suppose than to do. The soldier
seemed rather averse to degrade himself by contending
with Jamie, or even by touching him. " Do you take the
first shake ? " said he to Fleeman. " Na, na," replied Fleeman, " tak' ye the first shake, for fear ye getna anither;"
and he threw the soldier from him as he would have done
a child. Another and more powerful man shared the same
fate. The colonel now began to suspect that Udny's man
was better than he looked. He was likewise irritated by
the smiles which he saw playing on the faces of the bystanders, and he ordered out the best man in the regiment.
Jamie, too, was beginning to be in earnest. No ordinary
man could bear his powerful grasp, and the poor soldier
was dashed to the ground in an instant. Jamie now ran
up to Udny and inquired, " 'Od, have I a' that *dyke* o' men
to throw ? Tell their maister to send twa or three at a

time, or I'll be o'er lang in getting haine to tak' out the
kye." The Castlegate rang with shouts of laughter.

As Jamie lived a good deal at Slains Castle, and other
places whose inhabitants were rather favourable to those
who had espoused the cause of Prince Charles, and who
were hunted through every corner of the land by the
emissaries of the bloodthirsty Cumberland, he imbibed a
feeling of no very friendly nature towards "the red-coats."
In confirmation of this, we might relate two anecdotes,
both equally authenticated, but so similar that we think it
sufficient to give one. The circumstances on which they
originate took place at Udny market, and at Aiky Fair or
Old Deer. We give the latter. Jamie was at Aiky Fair,
and having met with a lad of his acquaintance, whom he
observed to be crying, he looked him earnestly in the face,
and in a tone of pity said, " I dinna like to see grown folk
greetin'. Fat's the matter?" The lad told him that one
of a recruiting party in the market had *trepanned* him, by
secretly slipping a shilling into his pocket, and then offer-
ing to swear that he was in possession of the king's money.
This was a practice of no rare occurrence in Scotland in
those days, and hence we are able to account for the circumstance of Jamie being several times engaged in a trans-
action such as we are now describing. If the poor fellows
who were thus unwittingly enlisted offered to remonstrate,
they were immediately reported as friends of the prince,
and enemies of the sovereign, and thus their last state was
worse than the first. Fleeman desired his acquaintance to
point out the fellow who had been guilty of such a disgraceful deed, when, taking the shilling, he offered it back
to the soldier. His Majesty's servant began to laugh at
Jamie, and told him he would enlist him next. " Upstarts
should be civil—tak' back your money," said Jamie; but

the soldier showing no disposition to comply with the request, Jamie threw the coin in his face. Had the soldier been wise, he would have carried the joke no farther; but, assuming a tone of great wrath, he began to threaten Jamie and his friend, and swore that he would make vengeance fall on the heads of such rebels. In an instant, Fleeman's "rung" was laid across the soldier's shoulders with such hearty good-will, that the poor "red-coat" reeled and fell. His companions, gathering round, seemed disposed to assist him; but the market people taking part with Jamie, the recruiting party, consisting of a sergeant and four or five men, were glad, after being rather roughly handled, to take a right sudden departure. Report says that, when they were scampering off, Jamie was capering in his usual way when anything pleased him, and muttering to himself these abrupt and somewhat unintelligible sentences, "Red coats and black coats nowadays fight under fause colours. They will a' be put to flight yet. 'Od, how they rin! Right never ran."

Jamie's genius was of a discursive stamp, and led him to various modes of employment. His biographer has neglected to mention one avocation in which he took particular delight. When a wedding or baptism among the gentry, or above all things of this description, the placing of a parish minister, was to be celebrated in the district of country with which Jamie was acquainted, he was sure to make his appearance on the day preceding the *fête;* but he came not to sit idle. He was employed in the capacity of a kind of under-cook, and considered it his peculiar business to turn the spit. Such was his predilection for this office, that during the latter part of his life, when winding-up jacks began to be used, he exerted his genius in no ordinary degree in contriving and executing devices

by which the obnoxious machine might be rendered use-
less ; and so sudden and unexpected were his attacks, that,
in general, no one could bring home the charge of the
jack's destruction to Fleeman. When the cooking was
over, and the company assembled, Jamie appeared in a
very different character. At the period when he flourished,
the country was infested with large gangs of strolling
vagrants or gypsies. Wherever there was a wedding, or
suchlike meeting, a number of these vagabonds was sure
to be present. It almost always happened that they became very unruly, and often excessively annoying to the
company. In some instances they carried their impudence so far as not only to mingle with their betters, but
to take the lead in the amusements of the day, and to
maintain their ground in spite of every remonstrance, and
in defiance of every threat. It was Fleeman's province to
keep these blackguards in order ; and so effectually did he
execute this office, that where he was present there was
never any annoyance on the part of the tag-rag-and-bobtail
gentry. They knew well that Jamie was armed with the
authority of the landlord, and as well that he would not
hesitate to exercise his commission with little respect for
their feelings, were they to encroach in the least degree
beyond the boundary to which he was willing to admit
them. In a word, there perhaps were few things in the
world of which those lawless banditti stood more in awe
than of Fleeman's " rung." Those who had felt its weight
knew its effects, and those who saw its size had some guess
what these might be.

C

CHAPTER V.

ANECDOTES AND WITTICISMS.

THERE are in the world some who make a great noise, have extensive influence, and consider themselves far removed from the ordinary ranks of life. It is sufficient to say that, strange and unaccountable though it be, many of them have scarcely any other way of making future generations aware that ever such men existed than to employ a painter, and get their picture hung up in the place where they think it will, in all probability, be longest preserved. They seem to have some strange forebodings that, with the destruction of the picture, the remembrance of their existence will be lost; and they cannot help occasionally thinking, that nothing will live on the breath of fame but distinguished merit or distinguished worthlessness. But a truce with these remarks. They may beget in the breast of some one who is now happy in contemplating the distinguished figure which he imagines he is making, a suspicion that an imperishable name is not to be acquired by assumed greatness or fortuitous influence, but by real merit or transcendent abilities; and we would not for the world deprive any man of his importance during the period of its natural or supposed existence.

It was attempted to haud down to future times the memory of Jamie Fleeman by the simple though common means now referred to, but Fleeman had no hand in this himself. On the contrary, it was with no small trouble, and by much skilful manœuvring, that a likeness of the fool could be obtained. An itinerant limner, named Collie, was for some weeks at Longside, in the way of his vocation.

This artist having by accident seen Jamie, was so struck with his singularly strange appearance, that he became desirous, above all things, to sketch his likeness ; but Jamie was of a restless turn, and scarcely ever remained in one position, even for a few seconds. Besides this, there was in his disposition a certain waywardness, which made him take great delight in frustrating the designs of all who in any way meddled with him. For these reasons, it was not till several plans had been tried and failed that the limner effected his purpose. One of Fleeman's favourites having got him into the inn at Sandhole, plied him with tobacco and ale, of both of which Jamie was remarkably fond. Word was sent to the painter that now was his time ; but the best opportunity is occasionally rendered unavailable by untoward circumstances. The painter had none of his tools at hand. Determined, however, not to lose the only chance which it was likely he would ever have, he drew upon his ingenuity to the account of his mishap, and made a piece of pasteboard and a burnt stick supply the place of canvass and brushes.* Keeping himself concealed in a corner, where he had a full view of his object, he contrived, with his rude implements, to produce a most striking likeness of Fleeman. The history of this rough picture is strange. The Rev. Mr Skinner of Linshart got it from Collie ; Miss Boyd of Ludquharn, afterwards Mrs Gordon

---

* We are under very great obligations to that eminent scholar and antiquary, John Leith Ross, Esq. of Arnage, for having put it in our power to present the public with a print of Fleeman. Mr Ross, on looking lately into some of his grandfather's repositories, found a bundle of drawings by Lady Mary Hay, which that gentleman had got from her ladyship about the year 1760. Among these was a likeness of Fleeman, done on a piece of stiff paper in pencil. This drawing exhibits all the characteristics of an original. It is from it that our print is copied. It is not improbable that this is the very picture which Collie drew.

of Wardhouse, having seen it at Linshart, begged it of Mr
Skinner, who made a present of it to her; but neither did
it remain long in her possession, for Lady Mary Hay, having seen it, pressed Miss Boyd so much to give it up, that
she consented, when Fleeman's picture graced the drawing-
room of Slains Castle, as its original often did the kitchen.
Whether Lady Mary took it with her when she married
General Scott, or left it at Slains Castle, we cannot tell;
nor can we tell whether it be still in existence, or whether,
like many things of more value, it has passed away on the
wings of time. Certain it is, that it was much prized sixty
years ago; but sixty years work wonderful changes. There
are many things besides Fleeman's picture that were much
esteemed in their day, which are now entirely forgotten or
held in utter contempt.

To try if Jamie was proof against the allurements of
pelf, some of his acquaintance about the place where he
was staying scattered a few copper coins in his way to the
well, and kept watch at the time when he was sent out for
water. Fleeman, carrying his buckets, came to the place
where the coins lay. Eyeing them for a moment, he said
to himself, loud enough to be heard by those who watched
his conduct, " When I carry water, I carry water—and
when I gather bawbees, I gather bawbees," and passed on.
This discloses a trait in Fleeman's character which we
greatly admire. It showed that he could not be allured
from his duty by the most tempting objects, and that he
thought it better to attend to the business in hand than
to turn aside to an entirely different pursuit.

Fleeman's wit was sometimes of a playful cast, sometimes of a grave and didactic nature, but in either case it
rarely failed to effect the object for which it was called
forth. A gentleman, whose drollery outran his prudence,

and who, perhaps, thought that his rank in life gave him a title to take any liberty he chose with one so much his inferior, having one day met Fleeman, asked him in a very pertinacious manner, " Who's fool are you ?" Jamie, eyeing him for a moment with a kind of odd stare peculiar to himself, and which seemed to indicate that he considered the gentleman's impudence to be fully as conspicuous as his good breeding, calmly replied, " I'm Udny's feel. Wha's feel are ye ?" It is needless to say that the laugh which the gentleman meant to raise at Jamie's expense was turned against himself, and he was taught the lesson, that the man who neglects the rules of propriety, in hopes that his rank will command the respect due to good breeding, lays himself open to the rebukes of those whose deference he would otherwise command, and reduces himself to a level with those whom he may thoroughly despise.

Being at Peterhead, Fleeman was one day on the shore near the " Wine Well," where several of the gentlemen belonging to the town were assembled, and seeing one of them with whom he was acquainted, looking very earnestly with a perspective glass at some distant object, his curiosity was excited. When with the naked eye he could see nothing very remarkable, he took the liberty of asking the gentleman what it was that he was so intensely surveying. " Oh, Jamie," said he, " I am looking at a couple of limpets that are trying a race on the Skerra !" * Fleeman, pretending to look for a minute with great attention towards the rock, remarked, " I canna just say that I see onything particular ;" but immediately turning up one side of his head, as if listening with anxiety, he all of a sudden assumed an expression of countenance as if he

* A rock in the sea nearly two miles distant from Peterhead.

had made some wonderful discovery, and, with an archness peculiar to himself, he looked the gentleman full in
the face, and with ludicrous gravity said, " L—d bless
me, sir, I hear the noise of their feet as they scamper up
the face o' the rock !" The gentleman had wished to
play off his wit on the fool; but the loud laughter of
those who were near plainly indicated that he had extremely little room to boast of his success.

Much in the same way did he silence a man who met
him one day near Waterton, and thought to play a little
on his credulity. " Ou, Jamie," said he, " have you heard
the news?" " Na, faith I," said Jamie, " fat news, man ?"
" Ou, that seven miles of the sea are burnt at the New-
burgh this morning !" " Od, little ferlie," replied Fleeman, " for I saw a flock o' skate, about breakfast-time,
flying past Waterton to the woods o' Tolquhon, maybe to
big there." In this way would he put to confusion those
who thought they might take the liberty of interfering
with him in a way which he did not think proper. His
replies on such occasions were so sudden, and so different
from what could have been anticipated, that they were
sure to confound his opponent and call forth the admira-
tion of the bystanders. As a farther proof of this, we
select the following anecdote from the number of his
graver retorts :—A young fellow, servant about a farmhouse where Fleeman sometimes staid a few days, had
seduced a poor girl in the neighbourhood. With an
effrontery not so common in those days as it has since
become, the rascal added to his first fault, not only by
resolutely denying that he was the father of the child,
but also by strenuously endeavouring to make it be believed that the girl's reputation had always been of a very
doubtful nature. As the girl was able to lead no collateral

evidence by which the charge might be brought home to him, he set her and the members of the Kirk-Session at defiance, and heaped no small abuse on them altogether. The poor girl, who, up to that time, had borne an irreproachable character, was much dispirited when she found the author of her disgrace also determined to impeach her veracity; for he again and again averred before the church court that he was ready to swear and prove to the world, as he said, that he was innocent, and that the woman was both a liar and a strumpet. When some years had passed by, and no confession could be drawn from him, the matter was at last referred to his oath, when, as far as this could do it, his character was cleared in the eyes of the world. But suspicion was by no means removed, for many were inclined to give more credit to the girl's word than to his oath, and several circumstances combined to prove that they were not mistaken. Some time after the business had been thus arranged, Fleeman paid a visit to the farmhouse. In the evening, when all were placed round the kitchen fire, the servants, as was common, were playing off little jokes upon Jamie, in order to get amusement by his quick repartee. No one teased him more than he who had so lately figured before the Kirk-Session. It was soon evident to all that this man did not stand high in Fleeman's estimation, whose growling laconic replies, or no less portentous sullen silence, gave him fair warning to desist from such a mode of amusement. But the fellow pertinaciously continued to tease the poor fool. " Jamie," said he, " ye're sic a feel, that I'll wager ye canna tell whether ye be your father's son or your mother's? Fat answer hae ye to gie? Come, tell me." And he burst out in a loud fit of laughter, as if he had got the better of Jamie. " Tell ye me first, then," said Fleeman, gravely, "fat answer ye hae to gie your Maker at the last day, when he asks you if ye didna break the lass' character, and then swear that ye did nae sic thing. It will maybe then be asked at you if ye can tell whether her boy be not your son as well as his mother's; and, faith, I'm thinking it will puzzle ye to mak it out that his being the son o' the ane hinders him from being the son o' the ither." It is needless to say that some laughed, and that some looked as if they did not know well what to do. But the upshot of the matter was, that, in the course of a few days after, the man waited on the minister, declared himself mis-sworn, confessed that he purposely endeavoured to injure the girl's character, and begged to be absolved from church censure.

Nothing provoked Jamie more than his auditors pre-tending, when he was relating some wonderful story, probably of his own invention, to be already intimately acquainted with all the particulars. On one occasion of this kind a person of the name of William Robb was amusing himself at Jamie's expense, by continually in-terrupting him, in the midst of one of his highest flights, with such exclamations as "Ou, I ken that!" &c. Jamie endured this for a time with some degree of equanimity; but at length, when he could bear it no longer, he took an opportunity of privately ascertaining the name of his tormentor; then turning to Robb with some asperity he said, "Dee ye ken, man, 't there's ane Sandy Robb, a brither or some near freen (relation) o' yours, gaun to be hanged at Banff on Munonday? I wager ye didna ken that." Robb was thus compelled to confess, amidst the laughter of those around, that Jamie's knowledge tran-scended his.

We have not been able to discover that Fleeman had

much sense of religious obligation. He had been brought up about the house of strict Episcopalians, and lived chiefly among those of this persuasion, and so was in some degree impressed with the notions inimical to the Established Church, of which the Episcopalians of those days were so much, and perhaps not altogether unjustly, accused ; but he did not carry his bigotry farther than an occasional sarcasm ; for, as often as he found it convenient, he attended the kirk of the parish where he was residing. In a word, his religious principles did not seem to give him much trouble ; but, when he was asked by any member of the Established Church how he, who was such a determined advocate of the Episcopalians, would condescend to enter a Presbyterian place of worship, he frequently would reply, in the most ironical tone conceivable, "he aye liket, in this matter, to be in the fashion wi' the multitude, whose religious principles depended on three things—what would gie greatest satisfaction to their friends, least trouble to themselves, and maist folk an opportunity o' seeing their braw claise." It was remarked that, when asked concerning the text, after being at the parish church, he invariably replied, " in the *tenth* of Ephesians." " And in what verse ?" the inquirer would ask. " Ye wish to ken a' things," Jamie would then say, "and therefore ye should be tauld naething. If ye get the chapter, there is but little fear but that you will meet with the verse." It is to be recollected that, in the epistle to which Fleeman directed those anxious to know the text, there are only *six* chapters.

About the middle of the last century, it was customary for the ministers of the Establishment to extend their discourses to an inordinate length, during which many of the congregation were often disposed to go to sleep. Fleeman, with that singularity which marked his character in most things, never gave way to the common failing, but seemed always to be paying the most marked attention to the sermon, however long or tedious it might be. In the Kirk of Udny, one Sunday—whether owing to the soporific nature of the sermon or manner of the preacher, we cannot tell—the disposition to slumber was greater than usual. Jamie was there, and, as was his wont, apparently all attention. The minister thought it necessary to admonish his flock with some severity. "My brethren," said he, "you should take an example by that fool there"—pointing to Jamie;—"fool though he be, *he* keeps awake while you —think shame of yourselves !—are nodding and sleeping." "Ay, ay, minister," muttered Fleeman to himself, "gin I had nae been a feel, I had been asleep tee." The *double entendre* and biting sarcasm of this brief soliloquy are inimitable.

In Jamie's day, field-preachings were of rather common occurrence at the "sacramental occasions" in the country parishes. Jamie, being present at one of these, saw many of those who had congregated behaving in a way not altogether in union with the pious motives which may be supposed to have brought them thither. Among other things, while the preacher was labouring to impart nourishment to their souls, they were busy taking refreshment to their bodies. There was perhaps little harm in this, and in the case of those who had come from a distance or from other parishes, there was a kind of necessity to be urged in favour of such practice ; but, on the other hand, there was certainly something rather unbecoming in the appearance of a set of people stuffing themselves with all kinds of food during the time of divine service, and we are therefore of opinion that there was room for reproof, as well as need for reformation, in this matter. Had the people been within the walls of the church, it is not probable that they would have indulged in such an unseemly practice; but being in the *field*, they considered themselves to be more at liberty, apparently unmindful that the sacred duties which they had come to discharge demanded equal reverence, whether performed within the walls of the kirk or under the broad canopy of heaven. But the plain truth is, that in those days the mists of ignorance were still hovering over the more sequestered parishes; many considered their presence at " an occasion" to be of more importance than the part which they took in the services, and believed that they had performed their duty by travelling a number of miles to hear an eminent preacher, and uttering an occasional groan during the sermon; while they seemed to think that there was little impropriety in eating and drinking, and smoking, and even sleeping, during part of the time they were there. Fleeman, fool though he was, highly disapproved of such conduct, and on the occasion alluded to sat with a face as grave as a judge, while numbers around him were busily and differently employed. At last a dog approached him, and from the expressions of kindness which the animal showed, it was evident that in Jamie he recognised an old acquaintance. Fleeman always kept a pocket well stored with bread and other eatables, and was never known to be sparing in his bounty towards the numerous curs with which he was in the way of meeting during his peregrinations. The dog in question tried various methods to excite Jamie's attention and to draw forth his bounty, but they were all in vain; Jamie sat unmoved. As may be supposed, the attention of many was in some measure engaged by Fleeman and the dog. At last Jamie held out his hand, and the dog, expecting to be treated as on ordinary occasions, approached nearer; but, instead of a piece of bread, he received a very smart stroke across the nose, which made him scamper off, yelping a very bitter complaint. "Tak ye that, ye ill-bred brute," said Fleeman, without relaxing his gravity in the least; "it will teach you better manners than to chew and eat in the *kirk.*" It is doubtful whether this sarcasm conveyed a severer animadversion on the practice of eating during the time of sermon, or of leaving the *kirk* to declaim in the *fields*. The only effect which it produced at the time was a titter which ran through the greater part of the congregation.

To an accident which befell him when following his avocation of cowherd, is to be ascribed the origin of a proverb very current in Buchan—"The truth aye tells best." Fleeman had, in repelling the invasion of a cornfield by the cattle under his charge, had recourse to the unwarrantable and *un-herd-like* expedient of throwing stones. One of his missiles, in an evil day and an hour of woe, broke the leg of a thriving *two-year-old*. Towards sunset, when the hour of driving the cattle to their home had arrived, Jamie was lingering by a dyke-side, planning an excuse for the fractured limb of the unfortunate *stot*. "I'll say," he soliloquised, "that he was loupin' a stank an' fell an' broke his leg. Na! that winna tell! I'll say that the brown stallion gied him a kick and did it. That winna tell either! I'll say that the park yett fell upon't. Na! that winna tell! I'll say—I'll say—what will I say? Od, I'll say that I flung a stane and did it! That'll tell!" "Ay, ay, Jamie," cried the laird, who had been an unseen listener to this soliloquy—" ay, ay, Jamie, the truth aye tells best!"

An anecdote related of Fleeman, in his office of guardian

of the geese, perhaps exhibits a mixture of the rogue with the wag. He had been sent to Haddo House to fetch some geese thence to Udny Castle. Finding the task of driving them before him a very arduous one, and his patience being completely worn out by the innumerable and perverse digressions they made from the proper road in which they should have walked, Fleeman procured a straw rope, and twisting this about their necks, walked swiftly on, dragging the geese after him, and never casting a look behind. What was his horror, when he arrived at Udny, to find the geese all strangled and stone dead ! As the breed was peculiar, the strictest injunctions had been given to him to be careful in conducting the geese safely home. His ingenuity soon devised a plan to free him from this dilemma. Dragging the victims into the poultry-yard, he stuffed their throats with food, and then boldly entered the Castle. " Well, Jamie, have ye brought the geese ? " " Ay, have I." " And are they safe ? " " *Safe !* they're gobble, gobble, gobblin,' as if they had nae seen meat for a twalmonth ! Safe ! Ise warran' they're safe aneuch, if they hae nae choked themsells ! "

The same ingenuity which he displayed in extricating himself from the scrape of the strangled geese he showed on another occasion. Loitering one day in the passage leading to the hall, while the servants were carrying in the dinner, his appetite was so strongly excited by the savoury smell of a couple of roasted ducks, that, watching a favourable opportunity, he pounced upon them, tore off a leg from each, and instantly devoured them. The servants discovered the theft, accused Fleeman, and insisted on his carrying the dish to the table. " These ducks, Jamie," said the laird, " are very queer ducks." " The deucks," mumbled Fleeman ; " what's the matter wi' the deucks ? "

" Why, they have only one leg each ! " " Ae leg ! od, there's naething queer about that. If ye look out at the window just now ye'll see the deucks in the yard in dizzens standin' upon ae leg, and what for shouldna these twa beasties hae but ae leg tee ? "

Fleeman was a good hand at repartee, nor were his powers of satire and quizzing by any means inconsiderable. It is recorded that one day, when travelling along the road, he found a horse-shoe. Shortly after, Mr Craigie, minister of St Fergus, came up to him, and Jamie, as he was acquainted with him, holding up the shoe, addressed him thus :— " Minister, can ye tell me what that is ? " " That ! " said the minister, " you fool, that's a horse-shoe ! " " Ah ! " said Fleeman, with a sigh—" ae ! sic a blessin' as it is to be weel learned ! I couldna tell whether it was a horse's shoe, or a mare's shoe ! " Mr Craigie, who delighted much in a joke himself, used to tell this anecdote with great glee, and remarked that wise men ought never to meddle with fools.

One year the Laird of Udny attended the " Perth Races." Jamie, as usual on such occasions, accompanied him. Taking a near cut across the country, he reached St Johnstone before his master. Having by some means got hold of the largest half of a leg of mutton, he had taken his seat on the bridge of Perth, and was making the best use of a large knife on the *lunch*, when Udny came riding up. As Fleeman had not often had such a joint of meat at his command, he had assumed no small consequence in his own eyes, as he sat refreshing himself like a prince. " Ay, Fleeman, are ye here already ? " said the laird. " Ou, ay," quoth Fleeman, with an air of assumed dignity and archness which no one could either imitate or describe, while his eye glanced significantly towards the mutton ;

"Ou ay, ye *ken* a body when he has onything." As much as to say, you recognise me as an acquaintance when you see me well provided with the good things of life; but would probably have taken no notice of me had I been less so.

The following anecdote displays a degree of good sense and courage which, perhaps, at that period, we should have looked for in vain from persons making greater pretensions to wisdom than "Feel Fleeman." Returning from Aberdeen one evening, Jamie, on arriving at the brig of Udny, found the road occupied by an appearance having all the characteristics of the enemy of man—long tail, hairy hide, and portentous horns. Fleeman attempted to pass this awful vision, but which side soever of the road he took Satan still confronted him. Fleeman dropped plump on his knees, and besought the foul fiend, saying, " O gweed deevil, let me past ! I'm naething but Udny's feel ! O gweed deevil, let me past !" But the "gweed deevil" was inexorable. "Be ye gweed deevil, be ye ill deevil," cried Fleeman with much indignant energy, as he began to gather an armful of stones, " Ise try you wi a *lea arnot !*" (a cant name for stones), and he commenced to pelt the "archangel ruined." Satan fled ingloriously, and in his flight dropped his hide, tail, and horns. Jamie soon after triumphantly entered the castle, and flung down the trophies of victory—the *spolia opima.* " Ye need never fear the deevil now, lads, for there's his skin," cried he in an ecstasy of delight. We question if the fellow-servant who personated his infernal majesty, would, if placed in Fleeman's shoes, instead of being disguised in the cow's hide, have acted with as much magnanimity.

A story tells that, on one occasion, being requested to deliver a message at some place several miles distant from

Udny, he took it into his head that he would not go unless
on horseback.   It was not thought proper to indulge him
in this luxury, and Fleeman, alive to a sense of the affront
thus offered to him, obstinately refused to go otherwise ;
when, at last, a servant luckily bethought himself of an
expedient.   He procured a stick, and giving this to Fleeman, said, " Here, Jamie, here's a horse for ye."   The fool,
with characteristic simplicity and great delight, instantly
bestrode the proffered stick, and arming his right hand
with a stout switch, gave his wooden steed a few stinging
blows, and darted away with great rapidity : and we may
well suppose that

> " The last of human sounds which rose,
> As he was darted from his foes,
> Was the wild shout of savage laughter
> Which on the wind came roaring after."

When Fleeman returned to Udny, he declared, " He's a
very rough rider yon beast ! Heigh, Sirs, I'm near as tired
as if I had ridden on John Shank's naig," which, being in-
terpreted, means " as if I had walked."

CHAPTER VI.

EXTRAORDINARY LIES.

THE extraordinary relations in which Fleeman occasionally
indulged, showed his love of the marvellous.   His talent
for lying was of the first order, and we have no hesitation
in placing him on a level with the highest geniuses of this
line.   His description of " a skate that wad hae covered
seven parishes, which he saw fleein' in the air," was an
idea equal to the best efforts of the great Munchausen, and

soars far above the happiest conceptions of Sir John Man-
deville or Ferdinand Mendoza Pinto. The story upon
which a very common byword is founded, "Hanging
in the weathercock, like Fleeman's mare," or, "Up by
carts, like Fleeman's mare," is nearly the same as one
recorded in the work of Munchausen. Being in Aberdeen ae snawy night, he said, he tethered his mare to
the lumhead, as he thought ; but a thaw having come
during the night, he in the morning found "the peer
beast hanging frae the steeple of the tolbooth.   Ay,
faith !" quoth Fleeman, viewing her, " Yir up by carts this
morning ! "

At the period when Fleeman lived, ploughs were generally drawn by oxen, and ten or twelve of these were
commonly yoked to a single plough. The oxen were
yoked by means of bows fixed on their necks, and the principal plough was held by the guidman himself, or by a
cottar retained for the purpose. To keep all the oxen at
work, a goadman was necessary. As this office seems to
have required some skill, the goadmen took great delight
in telling of the wonders which they had accomplished in
making the oxen to do their work. Many an old man yet
alive could recount feats of no common order which he
had made the oxen perform when he was a lad. Jamie
caught the infection, and seemed anxious that it should
be understood that he had been a first-rate goadman. But
if many verged on the very borders of truth and probability, exalting their character in this respect, Jamie took
a bolder step, and sought fame by relations altogether extraordinary. " Driving the oxen in the Laighs of Ludquharn," he said, " the ground was so swampy that he
often saw nothing above the surface but the nap of the

D

cottar's cap and the tap of the wyner's * bow;" and having quarrelled with the ploughman, who was ploughing one fine evening on the hill of Southfardine, he averred "that he drave the oxen at so brisk a pace, that the point of the share coming against a stone,† the ploughman's heels were, by the jerk which he received, made to fly up and strike the seven stars, when one of these brilliants was knocked down, and has never since been replaced."

But, fond of the marvellous himself, Jamie seemed to have a wonderful pleasure in repressing in others the least symptom of the same predilection, and, as if enraged at those who would dare to use the weapons which he considered as his legitimate property, he wrested them from their impotent hands, and made them heartily ashamed of themselves for having supposed that they could wield them. Sir Arthur Forbes of Fintray was the first in the country who introduced turnips into the list of their husbandry productions; and soon after the knight, the Laird of Udny turned his attention to the culture of the same useful root. As might be expected, much was said concerning the merits of the turnips, and the size to which they had been raised by each of these proprietors. One day, a person from Sir Arthur's neighbourhood having met Jamie, began to rally him on the superiority of the knight's turnips to Udny's. Jamie allowed him to go on till he had fairly described the wonderful size of the Donside turnip; and clearly perceiving that he had exaggerated in no ordinary degree, dryly replied, " Gang hame, man, and tell Sir Arthur, that Udny has made byres o' his neeps for his owsen. Ilka owse stands snugly in a neep, and eats

* One of the front oxen.
† A large white stone, still to be seen, we believe, is to this day known as " Fleeman's Stone."

round him for owks together, and, faith ! some o' the big anes would haud twa." The Donside braggart was silent.

It was customary, in Fleeman's day, for tailors to go round to the houses of their employers, and there to perform their work. The present practice of "taking in work" was scarcely known among country tailors sixty years ago. Prevailing practices are generally adapted to the circumstances or convenience of those among whom they are found. It was not till towards the close of the eighteenth century that the inhabitants of Aberdeenshire began to purchase cloth from the merchant. Every family manufactured what was necessary for its own use ; and when the web was prepared, the tailor was sent for, who came with his journeymen and apprentices, and remained till the work for which his services were required was completed. Thus, migrating from house to house, the tailors generally became a loquacious race, and delighted much in surprising their employers with wonderful narrations. A company of these tradesmen were employed in a house at which Fleeman chanced to arrive, and, as may be supposed, they were overjoyed when they saw the fool make his appearance. It was in the winter time, and a merry evening was anticipated. Many an incredible story was told by the tailors in order to draw Jamie out; and, it is said, he was not backward to enter the lists with his challengers. He heard their tales, and either told others which eclipsed their best narratives, or made such remarks as might have rebuked the narrators into silence. Perceiving that they could make nothing of Fleeman on ordinary grounds, his tormentors endeavoured to allure him into their own proper territory, no doubt thinking that they might then attack him with more success. One, addressing another, averred that, shutting his eyes, he could thread the finest needle half-a-dozen times in a minute. Another declared that, holding his hands behind his back, he could do the same thing. "I," says a third, "could promise to put a hunner needles on a thread in a minute, if onybody would hand me them." The master-tailor, with a leering look, and in a taunting tone, addressed Flee- man, "Could ye thread a needle, Jamie?" Fleeman, assuming a look peculiar to himself when a little nettled, or conscious of an affront, replied, with some warmth, " Ye wou'd like to ken, wou'd ye, tailor? Last winter, man, as I was passing Garpalhead, a ship was lying on the sands. She had been ca'd in by the storm, and she was loaded wi' needles. There were twa men wi' sho'els throwin' them out. Faith, I was wae to see sic a loss o' fine *sharps!* And spyin' a great clue o' sma' thread lyin'," quoth Flee- man, " I fell a-threadin' the needles, and I threadit as fast as the men could sho'el them out, an' I missed the deil ane! Great curse! that was a threadin' for ye !"

The allusion to the "Skate" is connected with one of Fleeman's outrageous lies. There lived in Jamie's day, and in the same district of country which he frequented, another fool named Jamie Tam or Thom, who also was noted for telling uncommon lies, and principally concern- ing things which he had seen. One day the two fools met by chance, and he in whose house the meeting took place, being a man of some humour, thought it a good oppor- tunity of ascertaining which of them would tell the most remarkable lie. Addressing Thom, he said, " Jamie, I'll warrant ye have seen some wonderful things in your day." " Ay," says Thom, " 'tis nae langer syne than yesterday that I saw red cabbage-stocks at Ellon so heich that nae- body could get up to them without a harrow." * Fleeman

* A harrow in place of a ladder.

eyed his brother fool with a look that bespoke a mixture
of contempt and consciousness of superiority, as much as
to say, " And is that the greatest lie ye can tell ?" And,
without the least pause or consideration, he began—" I've
seen a greater won'er than that mysel'. Ae day Countess
Mary was wantin' cockle-shells * to a gentleman's supper,
an' I gaed out to her Fish Peel † to tak' them, an' diving,"
said Fleeman, " I cam' to the boddom. Ye wou'd hae
thought it anither warl', man. An' sic fearfu' beasts as I
saw ! Gosh be here ! I was nearly fear'd out of my wit,
when a skate, that wou'd hae covered seven parishes, cam'
fleein' i' the air abeen my head ! Faith, I think I wasna
lang o' fillin' my creel wi' cockles, when I took to my heels,
an' never halted till I cam' up to the mou' o' the lang
haven." ‡ " The deil a marrow !" said Jamie Tam.

At times, when he heard any one relating a circumstance which set probability at defiance, he would listen
patiently till he had heard the whole, and then dryly ask
the narrator, " Do you ken where the leears gang ?" This
often produced remarks such as the following :—" Faith,
Jamie, I think there is no one that ought to know better
than you ; I'm sure you do not stick by the truth." " It
will never be ask'd at the like o' me," Jamie would retort,
" whether I spoke the truth or tauld lies ; but when wise
folk speak things that would affront feels, it is just makin'
a present o' their wit (reason) to Auld Bobby." Thus
would the fool reprove wise men.

* Oysters, we suppose.
† Alias, the German Ocean, which Fleeman often denominated
" Countess Mary's fish peel or pond."
‡ A creek running up between two rocks, close by Slains Castle.

CHAPTER VII.

GRAVE REMARKS.

A LITTLE acquaintance with the world will convince us that it is very possible for one man to ruin another, not only without having seriously intended to do him harm, but even without having ever felt any other sentiment towards him than that of kindness. There is a kindness which kills; and instances might be adduced, where marked attention could scarcely be construed into any other meaning than genuine cruelty. This can never happen but where the person on whom favours are heaped is in some sense unfit to receive them, and where the favours themselves have some tendency to bad consequences. One may be worthy of the most marked attention, and yet be unfit to be treated with too great kindness; for if he had not resolution to prevent the friendship of others from interfering with his duty, and to resist the various temptations to which certain modes of discovering kindness insensibly expose him, he may be ruined while he imagines that he is favoured, and lose his reputation while he believes that his company is prized. In such cases the attention of a friend almost assumes the nature of injustice, and his marks of kindness may be said to merge into acts of barbarity; for he fosters the bad propensities of him whom he pretends to favour, and leads him on to wretchedness under the banner of friendship. There lived in the district of country which Jamie Fleeman frequented, a farmer of very amiable disposition, but of little decision of character. This man, by steady attention to business and habitual economy, had raised himself

to comparative affluence. He was one of Fleeman's favourites. General Fullarton then resided at Dudwick. A
young officer, either an acquaintance or relative, occasionally paid a visit to the General, and often prolonged his
stay for two or three months at a time. This man was of
easy address and fascinating manners, and, from the account
which has come down to us, seems to have been what is
commonly called " a real kind-hearted fellow ; " but, from
the gay scenes in which he had mixed, and the example
which he had seen in the army, his moral principles were
not very high, and his habits, in one or two respects, re-
flected not much honour on himself, and were rather
dangerous to those with whom he associated. He would
not seriously have done or even wished ill to any man alive,
and yet there was a something about him which most of
men had cause to dread. Fond of fishing and coursing, he
occasionally invited the farmer whom we have mentioned
to accompany him in these sports. As they got better
acquainted they became more pleased with each other, till
at length they were almost inseparable companions. The
officer did not relish his sports so much if the farmer was
absent, and the farmer was unhappy when anything took
place to prevent his attendance. The farmer's enjoyments
were so multiplied by the officer's agreeable conversation,
that he soon began to feel little regret at leaving the dull
routine of business for pleasures so much more agreeable.
There was in the neighbourhood what was then termed " an
alehouse," where strong home-brewed beer and genuine
smuggled gin were sold. Hither the sportsmen generally
resorted some time in the course of the day. The officer
was generous, and seemed happy in treating the farmer
kindly in return for the time which he sacrificed. To make
a long tale as short as possible, the consequence of all this

was, that the farmer's affairs were neglected, and he con-
tracted a habit of drunkenness.   His wife and family endeavoured to break him off from this depraved habit; but he,
perhaps irritated by the consciousness of his own mis-
conduct, perhaps no longer capable of reasoning calmly on
any subject, resisted their attempts with indignation, and
seemed to consider their friendly endeavours as an encroachment on his liberty and a reflection on his good
sense.   Hence dissension broke out in the family; and
where peace and prosperity, respect and happiness, had been
—quarrelling, and confusion, and contempt, and wretchedness, in the course of a few years, took up their abode.
Fleeman paid a visit to his old acquaintance, and was
evidently sorry when he saw the sad change that had
taken place.   Instead of staying a few days as usual, he
prepared to take his departure in the course of as many
hours.   The farmer pressed him to prolong his stay, but
even fools can have little pleasure in the company of one
whose sole delight is to satisfy his own appetites, and
Fleeman would not consent.   " Na, na, " said he, in a grave
and melancholy tone, "na, na ; ae feel is aneuch at a time
about a house.   Feels, Robbie, canna bide lang in ae place.
Od, I'm fear'd ye'll shortly need to be trudging as well as
me."   Then, looking earnestly in the farmer's face, he
continued, " Did ever you hear, that for ae feel that God
maks, the deevil maks a score?   Faith, Robbie, I doubt
ye're auld Bruickie's handiwork," and having said this, away
he went without waiting for a reply.   Some time after,
Fleeman was at Dudwick, and by chance while he was
there the General's friend arrived.   Jamie generally claim-
ed the privilege of accompanying in their walks the gentlemen about whose house he was staying, and to this little
objection was offered, as all knew that Fleeman never re-

peated at one place what he heard at another. In the afternoon, the party at Dudwick were walking about the place, and having come in sight of the farmer's house, the officer made some inquiry concerning his acquaintance. The General, in few words, informed him of the man's altered habits. " I am sorry to receive such an account," said the officer ; " he was a good sort of man, and I should have been glad to hear of his success, but d—n the fellow, I could perceive when I was here some years ago, that he was getting too fond of the *Flushing.* I meant to have befriended him, but must now altogether cut his acquaintance." Fleeman, as was often his way, was heard making his own remarks on what had been said. " Od, some folk's friendship is like the auld smith's,* the less o't we hae the better for us." " What smith are you talking of, Fleeman ?" demanded the officer ; but Fleeman, nowise studious to give a direct answer, went on with his soliloquy ; " the mair he blaws, the sairer he burns, and then pretends to laugh at folk who say that wind blisters." " What can Fleeman mean ?" inquired the officer, looking at the General ; but Jamie proceeded : " Faith I believe it is soldiers' trade to kill folk : od, it would have been better for Robbie, and just the same thing to him, had he ta'en Robbie's life wi' his durk,† rather than wi' his kindness." " Fleeman," said the General, interrupting him, " here is a shilling for you to buy tobacco." Jamie thanked the General, and was soon on his way to Udny.

In Jamie's time, smuggling of gin from Holland was carried on to an almost incredible extent. From the Don to the Ugie there was scarcely a farmer or petty merchant

* A quaint term, by which Fleeman occasionally designated the enemy of mankind.

† His sword, we suppose.

within sight of the sea, who did not, more or less, engage
in this "free-trade" system. Illicit transactions generally
display very tempting prospects, but they rarely fail to in-
veigle their abettors into evils which lie deeply concealed;
so in the "gin trade," as it was called, men looked only to
the money which it promised to put into their pockets, but
considered not the neglect of more lawful employments
which it occasioned, nor the habits of intemperance and
immorality which it fostered. It placed immediately
within their reach the means of indulging to excess, and
to this they were tempted as often as they had occasion to
rejoice over a successful "run." When a cargo was safely
deposited, the partners in this speculation rarely failed
to make merry after their toil, and to dissipate over full
bowls that care and solicitude which had harassed their
minds during the time of landing and securing their
treasure. Hence many a sober and industrious man was
gradually betrayed into habits of inebriety and laziness.
Among others was one whom Fleeman had long known.
This man, previous to engaging in smuggling, had borne
an excellent character, but from that time he began to
neglect his business, and to become more and more attached
to his bottle. He still retained his obliging disposition,
which circumstance tended to render his debauched habits
a matter of very general regret. Fleeman was on a visit to
his friend, and as his remarks were generally as unexpected
as they were singular, he one day abruptly addressed the
farmer as follows:—"Od, Charlie, they say ye winna gie
Auld Nick a lodging ony way about your house, but just in
ae place." "I hope, Jamie," replied his friend, "he gets
nae encouragement to tak' up a quiet residence with me in
any place." "Faith, they say he does though," said Fleeman. "Od, man, I was tauld that ye let him lodge in your

gin bottle, and that ilka time ye taste the liquor, he comes
out into the glass and gi'es you a kiss. For the Lord's
sake, Charlie, tak' care o' him, he's a sleekit rascal ; and
guid faith, I've kent him bite aff three or four folk's heads
in his fits o' kindness." We have not heard whether
Jamie's strange rebuke had the least effect in making his
friend reflect on the dangerous course which he was pur-
suing. We suspect not ; for although we should imagine
that Fleeman's remark would have sometimes crossed his
mind when about to put the glass to his lips, yet we are
not ignorant how rarely it happens that one succeeds in
conquering a bad habit which he has allowed to acquire
strength. A confirmed drunkard, rather than relinquish
his bottle, would almost consent to salute Satan : and we
are of opinion that Fleeman got extremely little thank for
his remarkable advice.

Speculation is the greatest stimulus of improvement,
but it is likewise the means of hurrying many a man to
his ruin. If not pushed beyond rational bounds, it will
produce activity, and has every chance of being attended
with success ; but employed without prudence, and urged
without caution, its consequences will seldom fail to be
poverty instead of wealth, and ridicule in place of applause.
About the middle of the last century, speculation in agri-
cultural pursuits was scarcely known in the north of
Scotland. Many a good farm was then lying without a
tenant. Even the most unclouded prospects of success
could scarcely tempt farmers to hazard the smallest trifle
in improving either the soil or the implements of their
trade, and they were ready to predict speedy ruin to the
man who should have deviated in the least from the old
and rugged track. Men at a certain stage of knowledge
seem incapable of distinguishing between wild speculation

and rational enterprise, and are ever ready to dread the
consequences of the former, if any one recommend the
adoption of the latter. In this state was the great pro-
portion of the farmers of Aberdeenshire about a hundred
years ago. So very different was the system of farming
from that which now prevails, that scarcely a farm could
be found of which great part was not lying waste or
covered with morasses, and in few instances did the farmer
think it worth while to improve the one or drain the other.
What was still more extraordinary, if any one ever attempted to be a little more diligent than his neighbour in
correcting such errors, he was looked on by them with an
eye of contempt, if not of ill-will. They could scarcely
bear with patience to see any man departing from the old
system, which they held to be the best possible mode that
could be devised—a mode adopted by the wisdom of former days, and rendered next to sacred by long-continued
practice. The Laird of Udny was among the first in his
district who showed unequivocal symptoms of hostility
to this wretched system. Regardless of established customs
when not conductive to his interest, and of popular odium
when supported only by senseless prejudice, he adopted a
mode of farming so novel, and on so extensive a scale, that
the rustics stared with astonishment, and even ventured
to surmise that the lands of Udny could not long bear
such reckless expenditure. Fleeman heard their remarks,
and was deceived by their exaggerated representations.
Fearing that what all were predicting might prove true, he
resolved, like a faithful servant, to give his master a hint
of the issue in which his speculations were likely to ter-
minate. Watching his opportunity, he one day saw the
laird pointing out to a friend what he had already done,
and what he still meant to do on his domain. Fleeman

approached, and for some time seemed to pay great attention to what Udny was describing, then suddenly running
upon the top of a dyke, and there standing on tip-toe, he
looked around him with apparent anxiety. "What is the
matter now, Fleeman?" said Udny; "what are you looking for?" "Faith, sir," replied Fleeman, "I am looking for
places on which we may big win'-mills." "Windmills!"
said Udny; "what do you want with windmills?" "Od,
that ye may rid your head o' some o' them. Ilka body says
it's fou o' win'-mills; and, Lord bless me! how feared I
am, aye when the win' rises, they may turn your head
a'thegither; they will be your ruin." "Here is sixpence
for you," said Udny; "but recollect to keep in order the
blockheads who tell you these things, and not allow them
to speak ill of me or my plans either." Udny knew well
how to convert Fleeman's opposition into powerful sup-
port; for, after this, Jamie never failed, not only to ridicule those who spoke against his master's operations, but
also to maintain that "guid Udny" was setting an example
which every one who wished to become rich would do well
to imitate.

Most of people are as ready to give an advice to others,
as they are to consider whether it may not be partly appli-
cable to themselves. A rather curious instance of this is
on record, in which Fleeman acted a part. The Laird of
Udny had a friend in Aberdeen to whom he frequently
sent a present of game. Fleeman was generally the bearer,
and was not a little chagrined that he never received anything from the gentleman for his trouble. Deeming this
a departure from gentleman-like conduct, he resolved to
have his revenge by the neglect of every rule of common
courtesy. Being sent to Aberdeen with a few hares and
partridges, when he arrived at the house of his master's

friend, he stopped not at the door to give any intimation of his arrival; but, marching boldly into the apartment where the gentleman was sitting, threw the bundle on the floor, growled, "Hares frae Udny," and turned to go away. The gentleman called him back, gave him a long lecture concerning the importance of good breeding, and endeavoured to convince him of the rudeness and impropriety of his conduct on that occasion. Rising up, he said, "Allow me to tell you, Fleeman, how you ought to behave. When you come to the door of a gentleman's house, you ought not to walk in without farther ceremony; but, having knocked, ask if the master be at home; and having waited till he either calls you or comes to you, say, 'With his compliments, Udny sent you this bag of game, Sir.'" At the conclusion of this lecture, Fleeman suddenly took possession of his instructor's chair, and, assuming the air of a gentleman, said, in a very grave and dignified tone, "Give my best respects to Udny, and say I feel particularly indebted to him for his kind attention. And now, my good fellow," continued he, feigning to put his hand into his pocket, "here is half-a-crown to you for your own trouble." We have not learnt how the gentleman looked, or how he behaved on the occasion, but Fleeman certainly communicated to him the rather curious, though very important intelligence, that he who would offer an advice to another nowise indebted to him, must first bribe him to listen, otherwise the best counsel will be disregarded, and he who gives it considered officious and ill-bred.

At the time when Fleeman lived, religious controversy between those of the Established Church and those who adhered to Episcopacy prevailed to an extent, and was carried on with a degree of acrimony, to which we who

live in more peaceful times would scarcely give credit.
After the affair at Culloden, Episcopalians were looked on,
not only by Presbyterians, but by the government of the
day, as having been the principal friends and abettors of
the Prince, and therefore were considered as a dangerous
sect, which ought to be put down. These steady adherents
to a declining cause were disposed to search deeply into the
groundwork of their principles before they would consent
to purchase safety at the expense of profession; and having
satisfied themselves on this head, they exerted themselves
in no ordinary degree to keep their brethren from defec-
tion. None was more famous in this respect than Mary,
Countess of Erroll. She was in the habit of getting
prayer-books from London, and distributing them privately among her tenants. Such attention from such a
quarter had a most powerful effect in making them determined bigots, and they looked on danger as nought in
comparison of what they termed principle. Fleeman,
who allowed little to pass unobserved, was well aware
that a sure road to favour was to humour the foibles of
those whose good-will he sought. One day, when the
Countess was about to reward him for some important
service, he refused a pecuniary recompense which was
tendered, and begged that her ladyship would give him
a copy of "the prayer-buik." As the Countess knew that
Fleeman could not read a word, she was rather surprised
at such a request, and demanded of Jamie what he meant
to do with the book. Having satisfied her on this point,
he received a very neatly bound copy, and immediately
marched off to Whinnyfold, a fishing-village in the neighbourhood of Slains Castle. Here Barbara Fleeman,
Jamie's niece, had lately come to reside. Fleeman appears to have had a particular attachment to this young

woman, and, moreover, to have been of opinion that this
regard could in no way be more effectually proved than by
inducing her to become a bigoted admirer of the Countess
of Erroll and her religious predilections. But, as the sequel
will show, Barbara was not prepared to view these matters
in exactly the same light as her uncle. Fleeman found her
with two or three of her youthful companions who had
assembled to " weave a wedding " * in the evening. There
are many people who may be willing enough to acknow-
ledge a poor relative in private, but who are almost prepared to disclaim all connection or acquaintance with such
before the world. In particular, young people are apt to

* In the county of Aberdeen, about fourscore years ago, the manu-
facture of stockings, or "shanks," as they were provincially called,
formed the chief employment of women, and children of both sexes,
and even of many men, who thought it no shame to replenish their
purses by the proceeds of their labours in knitting during the winter
evenings. Crowds of young women frequently assembled to spend the
long evenings, when trials of speed in knitting, and "sang about,"
formed their employment. The "guidwife's" province was to keep
these young parties "in order," and to decide all matters with regard
to their work during the evening. In the "gloamin'," when the young
people were assembled, the goodwife sat down and measured off a
"wedding." This was done by putting all their "clues," or balls of
worsted, in a large dish, and unwinding from each as much as she
thought would employ "the lasses" for the evening. Exactly the
same length of worsted was unwound from each ball, and "a rose-
knot" tied. Sometimes the party divided into pairs for the contest.
If they all agreed to try at once for the victory, the goodwife mentioned some young fellow in the neighbourhood who was the known
sweetheart of some one present, or a general favourite with all ; or, if
they contended in parties, she named one for each. They all started
at the same time, and the young maiden who got first to the knot on
her worsted was allowed to indulge the hope that she would get for a
husband the youth who had been named. She who was accounted
his sweetheart wrought most laboriously to make good her claim ; and
the other girls, although they cared less for the young man, yet took
a pride in annoying their companion, and did everything in their
power to get at the "marriage knot" before her.

imagine that they would be disgraced by publicly recog-
nising a relative to whom nature or fortune has not been
over propitious. But, as the world is rarely ignorant of
the connection, such conduct tends rather to degrade
than to exalt them in the estimation of every one whose
good opinion is worth having. Barbara Fleeman received
her uncle with much coldness; but Jamie, not heeding
this much, took his seat among the damsels. After some
preliminary observations, he said, " Babie, ye're of the
gentle persuasion,* and I hae got the buik for you;"
and he at the same time drew the book from a fold of
his garment. " I'm gaun to the kirk" was the indirect
and laconic reply which his niece thought fit to make.
" Na, faith ye, lassie," said Fleeman ; " Ye can read, and
Lady Mary says that a' that read are o' 'the gentle persuasion.'" Whatever "the lassie" thought, she made no
reply, nor was it for some time that she took the book from
her uncle, holding it out to her. At last she snatched it
from him and threw it into the fire. Fleeman speedily
plucked it from the flames, and, looking his niece sternly
in the face, said, "I winna strike you, ye feel, and waur
than a feel. Ye think to affront me; I'm affronted wi'
you. Never call me your uncle, nor speak to me again."
Then relaxing from rage to grief, he said, " My heart was
leal to you, Babie ; but it can be sae nae langer. God for-
give you !" and, as our informant reports, Jamie was moved
to tears. His designs were completely thwarted ; his affec-
tions met with the most ungrateful return ; and poor Fleeman was overwhelmed with grief and disappointment. The
conduct of his niece was not to be commended, but a man
of ordinary powers of mind would have looked on all that

* A title by which Fleeman, from a wish to flatter the Countess of
Erroll and his other friends, generally designated Episcopacy.

she did as the thoughtless act of a foolish young girl, and after an admonition, would have thought no more of the matter; but to Fleeman's eyes it appeared a grave offence, which scarcely left room for pardon. Weak minds always invest trifles with an unbecoming importance. Fleeman muttered something about finding one who would both receive and respect his present, and took an abrupt leave of his niece. He never after entered the house where she resided, nor acknowledged her as a relative; and when he had occasion to speak of her, he called her "that woman." Barbara Fleeman, when arrived at years of more discretion, no doubt regretted what she had done in a moment of thoughtlessness, when surrounded by her youthful companions, and dreading their scorn on account of her uncle's kindness. In matters of much greater importance than this, a single rash or thoughtless action has not unfrequently been the cause of many evils, which regret can never wholly remove, and of disgrace, which time can with difficulty efface.

The person to whom Fleeman alluded as more worthy than his niece, was a girl whom he had supported almost from her childhood. She was an orphan, and Fleeman had found her, when very young, herding a cow. At that time she was crying for hunger, and in a very pitiable condition. Jamie ministered to her immediate wants from his pocket, and took such a lively interest in her favour, that he soon found means of supplying her with clothes. As he enjoyed a small weekly allowance from Udny, he contrived to maintain and educate this poor child, having placed her with an old woman, with orders that she might be taught to read, sew, spin, and knit stockings. Gratitude demanded of this girl that she should respect her benefactor, and she had good sense enough never to dispute the demand. She treated Jamie with filial regard, and he, in return, looked on "the lassie" with almost more than parental affection. When she was married, Fleeman gave her away; and it is said that, during the whole of the wedding day, he behaved with a degree of decorum and steadiness beyond what any one thought him capable of supporting. The only indication of a disordered mind which he betrayed, was his extreme solicitude that all things should be gone about in "*marriage order.*" * One

* To one acquainted only with the ceremonies of what may be termed a genteel wedding of the present day, the reason of Fleeman's anxiety about "marriage order" will be altogether unaccountable. It may be interesting to give a brief account of a country wedding, conducted according to the manner of former days. The bridegroom, when inviting his guests, always asked two young men to do him the favour to bring home his bride. These were termed "the sends;" he who was principally intrusted with the charge being called the "best send." He likewise invited two young girls to lead him to the place where the marriage ceremony was to be performed, and these were called "the bridegroom's maidens," the "best" and the "worst" respectively as each was to lead him by the "right" or "left" hand. In like manner, the bride asked two young men to lead her to the place of marriage; the one called "the bride's best young man," the other her "worst young man." She had likewise two young women termed her "maidens;" the one "the best," the other "the worst bride's maid." When the day appointed arrived, these repaired to the houses of the bridegroom and bride, respectively, as they had been invited, and at an hour rather earlier than the other guests. Their business was to see that the parties about to be wedded were neatly and properly decked out for the occasion. According to the time requisite for bringing the bride to the place appointed for the marriage, "the sends" took their departure from the bridegroom's house, and proceeded to that of the bride. Having arrived at the door, the "best send" knocked, and the bride, with her maids, having made her appearance, he asked, in case of not being acquainted with her, if she was the bride of such a man, and on her answering in the affirmative, he told her that the bridegroom had his compliments to her, and requested she would attend to the appointment agreed upon betwixt them at their meeting last past. He then saluted first the bride and then her maids, an example which was followed by his companion;

said to him, " Jamie, man, the bride owes you much."
" Her friends has paid it a' the day," replied Fleeman.

after which, the bride invited them into the house, where they were
treated with something to eat and drink ; and when there was music
and dancing, they danced with the bride and her best maid. That
done, they shook hands with the bride, mentioned the exact time that
the bridegroom expected her, and took their leave. Proceeding till
they met the bridegroom and his party on the way to the place appointed for the marriage, they reported to him that his request had
been complied with, and that his bride was a-coming. The marriage
ceremony over, the " sends " now lead the bride to her new habitation,
and the bride's maids lead home the bridegroom, while the bridegroom's
maids and the bride's " young men " generally walk in pairs. The person who first arrives is said to " win the brose." Having reached the
bridegroom's, some matron appointed for the purpose stood ready
with a basket full of " bun," or, in absence of this, of bread and
cheese, which being placed on the bride's head, the bun or bread and
cheese were broken, and handed round among the company. The
bride was then " welcomed " into the house by the bridegroom's
mother or some other woman appointed for the purpose, who generally took care to either compliment or taunt her according as the
match was agreeably to the friends or not. This matron then led
the bride to the fire-place, and gave her the tongs, by which ceremony
she was considered to be established in the possession of her house.
All now hastened to the dinner-table, at which it was considered altogether contrary to " marriage order," and even rather unlucky, if
the " officials " did not arrange themselves as follows :—The bride at
the head of the table ; on her left hand, first her best maid, then her
best young man, after him the bridegroom's second or worst maid,
and last of all the bride's worst young man ; and, on her right hand,
first the " best send," next to him the bridegroom's best maid, then
the " worst send," and, to the right of all, the bride's second maid.
Dinner over, the bride takes a glass in her hand, stands up, drinks to
the health of the company, then the bridegroom's best man or send
does the same, and, in the bridegroom's name, assures them of being
welcome ; after which the bride's best maid does the same thing, and,
in the bride's name, tells them that they are welcome guests. When
tired at the table, they rise to the dance. This, too, is a matter of
great ceremony, and four reels are completed before any of the ordinary company are allowed to begin. The fifth dance is always considered by the young fellows as a high honour, and is therefore sought
by every device, while not unfrequently the fiddler decides the mat-

On the man looking surprised, and remarking that he was not aware that she had any nearly related to her, Jamie said, "Poor thing, her good manners are her nearest kin. Faith! they have not proved bad friends to Mary, I think."

CHAPTER VIII.

HARDSHIPS AND DEATH.

THERE are few whose lives pass on from youth to age without misfortune and without trouble, and poor Fleeman did not escape the fate most common to mortals. The part of his biography which remains to be recorded compels us to leave the gay and frolicsome scenes in which we have hitherto found him mingling, and to accompany him into others of a sadder and more distressing na-

ter by declaring who has paid him for the tune. The dances arranged thus :—

1st. The bride is partner to the best send, and her maid to the other send.

2d. The bridegroom's best maid and best send, and bride's second maid and other send.

3d. The bride is partner to her best young man, and her maid to the bride's worst young man.

4th. The bride's maid and best young man, and the bridegroom's second maid with the bride's second young man.

5th. The bride and her maid, and any two young men of the company.

Before each dance, the men claim a kiss from their partners; and at the end of the first, third, and fifth dances, the bride and her maid tie a "favour" or blue riband to their partner's arm.

ture. In the early part of the summer, 1778, Jamie was one day exposed to a very heavy rain. As a poor wanderer rarely meets with much attention, so Fleeman found no kind friend who thought of giving him a stitch of clothes, or an opportunity of drying those which he wore. He arrived at one of his favourite haunts late in the evening. Drenched with rain and shivering with cold, he was, as usual, shown to his bed in an out-house. His constitution, which had long been proof against the worst usage, was, for the first time, forced to yield. He passed a sleepless night, and in the morning feverish symptoms were apparent. Had he met with the attention of any kind friend, he might have recovered; but of such he had none. All were glad to see him while he contributed to their amusement, and required not their aid; but now that he was incapable of the former, and stood in need of the latter, there were few whose pity he excited—few whose kindness he received. The world, taken as a whole, is selfish and ungrateful. There are many noble exceptions, but its general character is cold and unfeeling. It loads those with kindness who stand in no need of its favours, while it carelessly and cruelly overlooks those who would be glad of its least attention. While Fleeman could move their mirth, he was welcomed by all, and pressed to prolong his visits; now that he deserved their pity, he met with a cold reception from most, and none asked him to stay till he should recover his health. Jaundice succeeded to a severe cold, and Fleeman's robust frame gradually became weak and emaciated. In this diseased state, he wandered from house to house, till at last he reached Little Ardiffery, in the parish of Cruden. It has been remarked by some, that misfortunes, when they begin to appear, generally crowd thick upon each other. Poor Fleeman experienced the truth of this. Having taken up his lodgings for the night in the barn, he shook some straw on the floor immediately opposite the door. Before laying himself down on his humble couch, he secured the door by placing against it a large oaken plank, which he found in the barn. At that period there were no thrashing-machines in the country, and the servant lads had to rise early to provide provender for the cattle. In the morning, when Fleeman had fallen into a kind of slumber, the lads came to the barn door, and not recollecting that Jamie was there, they wondered what hindered the door from being opened, applied their strength to it, and, with a sudden jerk, overturned the plank which Jamie had placed behind the door. It fell with fearful weight on the poor creature's head, and not only cut him severely, but almost stunned him. He was able to crawl to a corner where the sheaves of corn were packed, and there he laid him down, weak from disease, and in pain from his wound. The blood continued to flow, but no one was present who sought to stem it. He was sick and parched with thirst, but no friendly voice spoke comfort— no kind hand ministered assistance. The servants plied their work, and thought little of the fool. The din of their instruments was incessant, although Jamie had never before stood more in need of quiet. In this state he continued till breakfast-time, when the lads having mentioned the misfortune with which he had met, Mr Johnston's daughters lost not a moment in showing him every attention, and administering every comfort in their power. The lads were not aware of the extent of the injury which he had received. They described the cut in his head as trifling; and, as they had heard of no complaints from poor Fleeman, they concluded that little was the matter. The young ladies were much horrified when they ascertained the extent of the wound, the quantity of blood which he had lost, and the feeble state in which he was. They had him immediately removed to the kitchen; and, as one of them was cutting off some locks of his hair, in order to have the wound properly dressed, he, for the first time, faintly exclaimed, "Alas!"

Poor Fleeman now felt that the cold hand of death was upon him, and he said to Mr Johnston, "When I am gone, ye winna lay me at Cruden; but tak' me to Langside, and bury me among my friends." Mr Johnston, perhaps not imagining that Jamie's death was yet at hand, replied, "Na, na, Jamie, we'll try you here first; and if ye winna lie, we shall then be forced to carry you across the hill." The tear came into the poor creature's eye, and he heaved a deep sigh, which made Mr Johnston repent of what he had said, for he plainly perceived that the time of jesting with Jamie was gone by. Fleeman, without saying a word, and in spite of every remonstrance, prepared for his journey to Longside. He thanked those who had shown him kindness, and said he forgave every injury which he ever had received. Then summoning the last remains of that strength which for many a day had enabled him to consider all ordinary exertion as nought, he found it scarcely sufficient for the task which he had now to perform. The distance which he proposed to walk was about eight miles. This, at one time, would have soon been gone; but now it was the work of a whole day. He found it necessary to call at every house in his way, that he might rest his weary limbs, and often had he to sit down on the road-side for the same purpose. A month previous to this, and he was scarcely aware that the vigour of youth had left him; now he found himself labouring under the imbecility of extreme old age. Such are the sudden changes which disease can produce—the direful effects which the neglect of the ordinary means of preserving health may cause. The shadows of the evening had fallen thick before Jamie reached his sister's cottage at Kinmundy. Martha prepared a bed for him, on which he might wear out his remaining days. They were not many. On the second, his strength was so far gone that the neighbours were called in to see him take his leave of the world. While standing round his bed, one said to another, "I wonder if he has any sense of another world or a future reckoning?" "Oh no, he is a fool!" replied the other; "what can *he* know of such things?" Jamie opened his eyes, and, looking this man in the face, said, "I never heard that God seeks where he did not give." The bystanders' unseasonable reasonings were cut short. Fleeman lay quiet for a short time, when he again opened his eyes, and looking at one whom he respected, and who stood near, he said in a firm tone, "I am a Christian, dinna bury me like a beast." * These were his last words. In the course of a few minutes after he had uttered them, he quietly breathed his last.

His funeral was numerously attended. The Messrs Kilgour at that time employed a number of wool-combers and weavers at Kinmundy, all of whom they sent to assist in carrying the body of Fleeman to the grave, and they generously treated those who attended the funeral with porter and cakes; so that the poor creature, who died almost friendless, had a decent burial. His remains lie near the north dyke of the churchyard of Longside. No stone marks his grave; but some years ago, when we were

---

* One yet alive, who resided in Kinmundy at the time, says Fleeman's last words were, "I'm of the GENTLE PERSUASION, dinna bury me like a beast."

there, and the spot was pointed out to us, a bush of broom waved gently over his ashes.   With the exception of some old people, few could now point out the spot where the remains of him who was once so widely known repose in the silence of death—so soon is man as if he had never been ; and the merry and the grave, the wise and the fool, are in this alike.

THE END.

PRINTED BY WILLIAM BLACKWOOD AND SONS, EDINBURGH.